SMITTEN AT CHRISTMAS

Amish Romance

HANNAH MILLER

D1519950

Tica House
Publishing

Sweet Romance that Delights and Enchants!

Personal Word from the Author

To My Dear Readers,

How exciting that you have chosen one of my books to read. Thank you! I am proud to now be part of the team of writers at Tica House Publishing who work joyfully to bring you stories of hope, faith, courage, and love.

Please feel free to contact me as I love to hear from my readers. I would like to personally invite you to sign up for updates and to become part of our **Exclusive Reader Club** —it's completely Free to join! Hope to see you there!

With love,

Hannah Miller

**VISIT HERE to Join our Reader's Club and to Receive
Tica House Updates:**

https://amish.subscribemenow.com/

Chapter One

Sunlight filtered in through the gap in the curtains of Rebecca's small, undecorated room. She opened her eyes and sat bolt upright. She had overslept. She swung her legs out of bed and into her slippers and hurried, still in her nightdress, down the hall and into Esther's room. The old woman set down the book she'd been reading and glowered at her.

"What time do you call this?" she snapped. "I've been lying here for hours."

Rebecca doubted Esther had been awake any longer than forty minutes or so, but she didn't argue. Instead, she helped Esther out of bed, massaging feeling back into the woman's cold feet before helping her stand. Esther then shrugged out of Rebecca's grip and made her own, slow way to the bathroom.

After toileting, Rebecca helped Esther wash and then dressed her. The old woman's fingers were swollen and bent, and she struggled to lift her arms over her head. Dressing her was slow, but they had long since gotten into a rhythm that meant it didn't take as long as it used to.

At first, Esther had resisted much of Rebecca's help, despite paying her for it. Now, she accepted the daily routine they had gotten into, more or less. Occasionally, she still snapped at Rebecca for being too rough or not fastening her *kapp* exactly right. Today though, there was more grumbling than usual.

"Silly girl," Esther snapped. "This apron has a smudge on it. Find me another and wash this one."

Rebecca bit back a frustrated sigh and did as she was told. She knew Esther's bad mood was her own fault for sleeping in. Usually, her internal clock was far more reliable than any other, and she never set the alarm on the little wind up clock her father had given her one Christmas. Today, however...

Today was off to a bad start. She just had to hope it would get better.

It didn't. After washing Esther's clothes and hanging them out to dry on the lines in the basement, Esther demanded she weed the barren front flowerbed, despite the dark clouds threatening rain. Isaac Farmer usually did the beds, but he was in his sixties himself and had come down with the flu last week. Not to mention, who weeded flowerbeds in the late fall? It was absurd, but Rebecca had learned long ago not to argue with the woman.

After coming back inside, she made Esther a cup of nettle tea, helped her to the toilet, and made them both a quick lunch. Esther was content to sit with her darning for a while, only occasionally complaining about the arthritis in her fingers. It was a warm day, not very cold for late November, and the fire was going in the warming stove. Esther's arthritis was more or less leaving her alone today, which was a blessing for them both. Making sure Esther had a glass of water and a book on the table beside her, Rebecca fetched her bicycle from the barn and fastened her basket to the back. She checked the tires, and finding them still inflated with no punctures, she set off toward town.

They needed several things—more thread, soap, and sugar. Not to mention feed for the chickens.

Rebecca disliked the chickens that roamed about Esther's property, half-wild. Only yesterday the largest of the hens had come running at her. Of course, hens had no talons, but this one had gotten in a few sharp pecks at Rebecca's ankles. Esther, however, loved to sit outside amongst them, weather permitting. She had names for them all and clucked as though holding a conversation with them. None of them ever pecked Esther. Half of them didn't even lay eggs, but Esther refused to get rid of even the most useless of them. Rebecca was pretty certain Esther preferred the company of her precious chickens to the company of most people, and certainly more than Rebecca's company.

Rebecca hadn't wanted to move in with Esther. She'd taken the job on the condition that it was a day job. At first, it had only been afternoons—to cook and clean and run a few errands. Then it had become an all-day job, and, as of last month, Esther had asked her to move in.

Rebecca earned a decent wage, at least—Esther had increased it as the work had increased, and Rebecca was grateful for that. But the woman was demanding, and Rebecca missed living with her family, with her mother and father and sister. Still, at least it was only a couple of miles to her family's home from here, and she still got to see them many days. She even had a couple of afternoons off a week to spend with them.

Esther didn't live too far out of town either, just three and a half miles. With the bicycle, Rebecca reached Bungler's Hill in no time at all.

Their town in Illinois was small, with only a few old buildings left to give it some character. Rebecca liked being here, liked watching people come and go. But she didn't have time for leisurely people-watching today. Often, she would take her time, browse the shops a little, sit in the park and throw seed out for the ducks. But she'd risen late, and the day was getting on. She still hoped to have all her chores done by evening and be able to join her family for supper.

The weekend market was the perfect place to find what

she needed—and the perfect place for distractions. Despite the promise to herself to make the trip a quick one, she found herself looking at snow globes and hand-carved wooden boxes she had no need for. She didn't buy them though—she'd always been sensible that way, she supposed. Never frivolous, unlike her friend, Mary Joan, Rebecca thought with a smile as she spotted her friend a few stalls away, handing her money to a vendor with a smile and a nod.

Rebecca wandered over to greet her, and Mary Joan smiled widely. She had a beautiful smile, one that always made Rebecca's lips twitch upwards, no matter how bad a day she'd been having.

"Are you well?" Mary Joan asked. "I feel as though I've not seen you in forever."

"Well enough, thank you," Rebecca said. "Although Esther has been running me ragged lately."

"Is she worse? I can't say I like her very much, but I do hope she's getting along."

"Some days are better than others," Rebecca said. "She might improve when the weather turns warmer, but that won't be for a long while. Her hips are troubling her at the moment." And her hands, and her knees, and her memory, Rebecca thought but didn't say. Rebecca knew Esther wouldn't like her discussing her ailments with anyone, and even though it was only Mary Joan, Rebecca wanted to respect the woman's privacy—she knew she would expect the same if she were in Esther's shoes.

"*Ach*, look," Mary Joan said suddenly and grabbed Rebecca's arm. "It's Daniel Shrock. I mean, *Mr.* Shrock. Oh, he's coming this way."

All thought of Esther fled Rebecca's mind. Rebecca could only stare as Mr. Shrock walked toward them. He nodded to them and tipped his hat. "Good day, ladies," he said.

His voice was like honey, Rebecca thought, smooth and sweet. Rebecca almost wished he'd been a teacher at school when she was there—she could listen to that voice all day long, she thought. The only male teacher for some time, Daniel Shrock had made quite a stir when he'd moved to their district.

He was handsome, too. Rebecca liked his eyes, dark green and warm, with creases at the corners. His jaw was strong, his lips ample, and his hair fine gold.

"Good day," Rebecca managed, her voice coming out a little weak.

"What brings you to town?" Mary Joan asked, her voice not failing her even a little.

"Oh, I'm just running a few errands. Nothing very exciting, I'm afraid."

"Same here," Rebecca said, although he hadn't asked. "Just refilling Esther Fretz's pantry."

"*Jah*, how is dear Esther?"

There was no hint of irony in his voice, and it struck Rebecca as odd to hear of Esther being referred to as 'dear'. Few people in the community got along well with her these days, although she still commanded respect.

"Not so bad," Rebecca said carefully. "She's a little fragile, but she manages along well enough."

"I suppose she does," Mr. Shrock said. "She's a tough lady. I knew her son and his family from Indiana, you know. Wonderful people. Very giving."

Rebecca's eyes widened. "Did you really?" she asked. "What a strange coincidence."

"Well," Mary Joan said with the edge of laughter to her voice. "Everyone knows everyone around here. I suppose it's just the same there. Not that much of a coincidence really."

"*Nee*," Mr. Shrock agreed. "Not much of coincidence, I'm afraid. Mind you, I really should stop by Esther's place soon, check in on her. Although I'm sure you're taking excellent care of her."

Rebecca beamed at the praise, her heart fluttering a little. "I do hope so," she said.

Mr. Shrock told them then that he had to be on his way—and on his way he went, with a courteous goodbye.

"Isn't he *gut*-looking?" Mary Joan said with a sigh.

Rebecca didn't reply to that. She wasn't anywhere near as outspoken as her friend.

They continued to shop together for a short while, but Mary Joan lingered too long at each stall, and Rebecca had to excuse herself. She wanted to finish her shopping and get back to Esther.

But when she returned to the farmhouse, the old woman was singing to herself. Not only that, but she was in the kitchen, baking a pie.

"It's going to look awful," Esther muttered to Rebecca when she noted her presence. "I couldn't mix the pastry quite right. Can't for the life of me remember the recipe, but never mind. For the two of us, it should be all right."

Rebecca smiled. She hadn't seen Esther make anything more taxing than a cup of tea or pre-made soup in weeks. Nor had she seen her in such good spirits. Rebecca hurried out to check on the chickens and scatter feed for them before locking up the coop, and then she returned to check on the pie. It was almost done, but when Rebecca informed Esther, the old woman only frowned.

"Pie?" she asked. "What pie?"

Rebecca sighed. Esther had been forgetting things like this for a few months now, and Rebecca worried about it. The doctor had said it was merely old age, but Rebecca didn't like it one bit.

"*Ach!*" Esther cried, then, as though Rebecca had never reminded her. "My pie!" She pushed herself to her feet.

Rebecca followed her into the kitchen, turning the oven off for her once she'd taken out the pie. The pastry looked a little tough, but not too bad, and it smelled wonderfully sweet of cooked apples and cinnamon.

Rebecca busied herself making a quick stew for Esther after that, something a little more substantial than pie for her supper. There were leftovers from it, too, something for lunch tomorrow, to make things easier. Once Esther had eaten and had settled herself down with a book, Rebecca excused herself and fetched her bike once more.

Her family lived just a mile down the road, so the ride was a short one. Her sister, Iris, was on the porch with her sewing when Rebecca arrived home. Despite the earlier dark clouds, the afternoon had transformed into a cool, clear day for mid-November, and Iris was clearly making the most of it.

Despite living at Esther's almost full time, this sprawling white farmhouse was still her home and always would be. It smelled warm and inviting, of the basil and rosemary that always sat along the kitchen windowsill. Today, it smelled too of roasting vegetables and chestnuts.

Iris didn't embrace her—that wasn't Iris's way. Rebecca loved her sister, but the younger woman was cold in manner if not in heart. She nodded to Rebecca and picked up her sewing from the seat beside her so Rebecca could sit.

"How have things been going this day?" Rebecca asked. She knew Iris would never initiate a conversation—Iris had always been too much in her own world, uninvolved with the lives of others. Rebecca wondered if she would ever marry—it would take a strange man to make a wife of Iris Beck. As far as Rebecca knew, Iris had never been courted by anyone, nor ever been interested in courting anyone, although she was now almost twenty.

"Same as usual," Iris told her. "One of the goats got out last night. Father's hoping he'll come home by himself. He went out in the pony cart but couldn't find him anywhere. And Doris died Thursday night."

"Doris?"

"The speckled hen," Iris said. Iris was almost as bad as Esther when it came to those birds. She named every one of their animals, even though father had always scolded her for it.

"*Ach*," Rebecca said with sympathy. "I'm sorry. I know you liked that one."

"She was my favorite," Iris said, her tone unchanging.

Rebecca nodded. "How are *Mamm* and *Dat* doing?"

"Well," Iris said, still focused on her sewing. "*Mamm*'s in the kitchen. I've no idea where *Dat* is though. I think he might have gone next door."

Next door was the Lapps' family home. Now in their

seventies, *Dat* was often round there to help with their chores. Sometimes Rebecca's brother, James, would go round to help too, although not as often. He had his own small-holding now and a six-month-old son to care for. Rebecca doubted they would see him at dinner tonight. Still, James was Rebecca's favorite sibling, and she always hoped to see him, even if it was something of an unlikely hope.

Dinner was a little later than usual—*Dat* had lost track of the time and in the end, Rebecca was sent to fetch him. He'd smiled when she'd approached him, and she'd had to duck out of his reach to avoid him staining her clothes with his earthy hands. Not that she would really mind if he gave her a hug— mud and dirt were things Rebecca was all too used to.

Finally, later that evening, she bid them all good night, and although she told them she was perfectly fine cycling back to Esther's, *Dat* insisted on driving her in the buggy. Rebecca couldn't deny she enjoyed the time spent with him, even if he did most of the talking—going on about the different types of nails they were using to build the Lapps' new barn.

Esther was still awake when Rebecca got to the house. Rebecca found, even after a month of boarding there, that she couldn't think of this place as home. It was Esther's home, not hers. *Her* home would always be her *mamm* and *dat*'s house.

She helped Esther undress and helped her get into bed,

fetching her a glass of water for her nightstand and then bidding her good night.

Rebecca lay awake for a while after that, unable to shake the homesickness that still plagued her. Eventually, after much tossing and turning, she slept.

Chapter Two

Rebecca woke early the next morning, as though her mind were making up for the day prior. She washed and dressed and went to put on the tea before knocking on Esther's door. Esther called for her to come in, and Rebecca did so. The old woman pushed herself up to a sitting position, and when Rebecca offered her arm, Esther took it and eased herself out of bed. Rebecca helped to dress her, commenting on how nice the day outside looked.

"Hah," Esther responded. "I can feel in my bones there's nothing 'nice' about the weather today. Have you lit the fire in the front room?"

"Not yet, but it's quite warm in the kitchen. You can sit in there while I get the fire going."

The kitchen of Esther's home was a small room with

uncomfortable wooden chairs. Esther more often took her meals in the sitting room at the front of the house, where the windows looked out onto a big, gnarled oak tree that sat at the end of Esther's property.

Rebecca poured Esther her tea and laid out the breakfast things for Esther to help herself to, and then hurried into the sitting room to light the fire. Rebecca's family home had only gas stoves, but Esther used a wood burning stove in the kitchen and an old-fashioned fireplace in the sitting room. It was an aspect of Esther's home that Rebecca rather liked. The whiff of woodsmoke was comforting.

After breakfast, Esther sat to read in the sitting room for a spell. She was complaining about her hands—the day *was* cold outside, and cold made Esther's arthritis all the worse. Rebecca felt badly as she saw Esther struggle to turn the page of her book, her hands gnarled and swollen.

Rebecca went out to the chickens, feeding them and letting them out of her pen. She threw a little extra straw into their coops in case they were cold and left them to their scratching and clucking.

The post had arrived by the time she was done, left on the little table on the porch. She hadn't heard the sound of the knocker, if the mailman had indeed knocked at all—he often didn't. In truth, it was only for Esther that the postman actually came right up to the house with the mail. Everyone else got theirs in their mailboxes by the road. Rebecca often wondered about it, knowing that somehow Esther and the mailman had a special friendship.

She flipped through the letters to make sure there were none for her and then took them into the sitting room. She was about to set them down on the table for Esther when she realized Esther probably wouldn't be able to open them with her hands aching the way they were. She opened the first one and handed it to Esther.

"Oh," Esther said, peering at it. "It's from my son, John. He has such terrible handwriting. I don't know where he got it from. His father's fault, I expect. You'll have to read it for me. I can't make head nor tail of this chicken scratch."

Rebecca bit back a smile—Esther's insults were more humorous when they were directed at someone else, she found. She began to read it aloud.

The short of it was that Esther's son wanted his mother to visit for Christmas. He talked of how the children were doing, and a little of life in Baker's Corner, Indiana, although his letter was only a page and a half long.

"Visit Indiana? What nonsense," Esther muttered. "He should never have moved so far away. My late husband told him as much at the time. He told him, at his later regret, that we would not be visiting. Of course, I always thought Jordan might come around one day, and we'd visit John together, but..."

"Perhaps your son could visit you here?" Rebecca suggested.

Esther shook her head. "I haven't enough space for them all, and that wife of his would never spend Christmas away from her own family, certainly not for my sake."

Rebecca could understand that. Maybe Esther was nicer to her family than she was to Rebecca herself, but she rather doubted that clipped, no-nonsense manner of hers ever eased the slightest bit.

"It would be nice to see my grand-*kinner*, though. Why, I haven't even met the youngest two, and Bobby was still in diapers when I last saw him. That was the last time they came to visit me. Getting on ten years, it must be now..."

Rebecca bit her lip. She knew that if Esther wanted to go, she would have to go with her, for she couldn't let Esther make the journey alone. But it would mean leaving her own family, spending Christmas with only cranky old Esther and her family—people Rebecca had barely even heard of before now.

She didn't want to go. She wanted to stay here and make Christmas decorations with *Mamm* and Iris and watch the school presentation with Mary Joan and compliment Mr. Shrock on how well it had all come together. Perhaps Mr. Shrock would even ask her...

She pushed that thought to the back of her mind as Esther folded the letter and said, "I'd like to go visit him. Rebecca, help me write out a reply, and then we'll start to make arrangements."

There was no asking. That was the worst thing. Esther could have at least *asked*, pretended as a courtesy. Instead, there were only commands and the implicit assumption that *of course,* Rebecca was coming, carried along like a useful piece of luggage.

Rebecca held her tongue and nodded and went to fetch paper and pen. Esther's hands shook too much these days, and her eyesight was poor, so she dictated while Rebecca wrote. And there it was, "*My helper, Rebecca Beck, will be accompanying me and will need to be accommodated.*"

And least, Esther had thought of accommodation. At least, she wasn't merely being thrown in some dark closet with the rest of the luggage.

It was done, she thought. She had little choice in the matter. She couldn't deny Esther this, and she knew Esther would not undertake the journey alone, *couldn't* undertake the journey alone. Rebecca knew what her mother would say—that it was Rebecca's Christian duty and obligation to accompany Esther.

Later that day, Rebecca took time out of her errands to make a visit home. *Mamm* did not surprise her.

"I know it's not easy, daughter, but if it's Esther's wish, you have to help her. She can't go by herself. I'm sure you know this already, but she's an old woman. Help her see her son. It might be her last chance to do so."

Rebecca sighed and leaned back slightly in her chair. Her helping of apple cobbler was almost untouched.

"It's going to be awful," she complained.

"You'll get through it," *Mamm* said. "You have many Christmas seasons ahead of you to enjoy. Esther does not."

Rebecca knew she was looking for sympathy in the wrong place. If she wanted sympathy, Mary Joan was the person to talk to, not *Mamm,* not *Dat,* not even Iris. But *Mamm* was right, Rebecca knew that, too. She might have taken the job as Esther's caregiver for the money and what she'd thought then was independence, but she stayed because Esther was part of her community and needed someone to look after her.

That someone was Rebecca. Even if Rebecca wanted to end her employment with Esther, now wasn't the time. No, she would have to go. Perhaps it wouldn't be as bad as she feared...

Chapter Three

They hired a van to take them to Baker's Corner, Indiana. It was a novel way to travel for both of them, but for the length of the journey a horse and cart would never do and would have made the journey impossible for Esther. Modern conveniences were a fact of life outside of the Amish communities, Rebecca thought, and on rare occasions, it could be considered acceptable to take advantage of them, so long as they did not *rely* on them. Of course, not everyone felt the same about that, but no one was going to argue with Esther. Rebecca was simply along for the ride.

Rebecca didn't need to take much luggage—she had only a single suitcase, while Esther had two. The old woman was rather attached to material things, but Rebecca knew that was just because she was nervous about leaving home. She wanted to recreate that sense of comfort when they got to Baker's

Corner, and so Rebecca hadn't argued about packing the old Bible or the small clock that had once belonged to Jordan Fretz, Esther's late husband.

The journey was a lengthy, longer than all Rebecca's buggy trips, and she was grateful for the van's smooth drive rather than the rattle and sway of a buggy. She thought Esther was probably grateful for that too, although she still complained of aching limbs from sitting too long in such a small space.

The countryside passed them by, hills and rivers and woodland and farms, small towns nestled amongst them all. Rebecca dozed a while, only waking when the driver stopped the van at a small, rather run-down looking gas station. Rebecca climbed out of the van and helped Esther out to visit the bathroom. It was good to stretch her legs, and Rebecca nosed around the little convenience store without buying anything (she had packed sandwiches that morning), while the driver paid for the gas.

Then they were back in the van, and it was Esther's turn to doze. Rebecca listened to the radio and chatted with the driver a little.

And then they were there. *Welcome to Bakers Corner.*

Five minutes later, the driver pulled up outside a smart white farmhouse, slightly back from the road down a quarter mile of dirt driveway. The sun was setting, and a woman emerged from the house. She waved, and Rebecca waved back. She nudged Esther gently to wake her, and the old woman snorted and uprighted herself from her slightly slumped position. The door to the house opened again, and a small horde of children came streaming from it, followed by a man with thick black hair and a long black beard.

Rebecca helped Esther down from the van and greeted the family politely. She glanced at Esther and wondered if she had ever seen the old woman look so happy. Esther rarely smiled at anything, but she was positively beaming now. She embraced her son, and greeted her grandchildren warmly, commenting on how tall they'd grown, and how much the eldest boy, Harry, looked like his father. Then she introduced Rebecca to all of them.

Looking at the elder of the two girls, Rebecca could see some similarities between her and Esther herself—something in the line of the jaw, and the sharp slope of her nose. The girl looked far too serious for thirteen—which Rebecca knew she was, but her older brother had a cheeky grin that Rebecca found endearing. The younger of the five children were more reticent to come forward. Sandy, who was six, stayed close to her mother, while the youngest, Ross, begged to picked up by his father, who complied. Still, they smiled and laughed when Esther pinched their cheeks and ruffled their hair. Sandy seemed more interested in Rebecca, though, staring at her with wide, brown eyes, almost unblinking. Rebecca smiled and nodded at her, and Sandy nodded back shyly.

"Well, let's go inside," Debbie, John's wife, said finally. "You've had a long journey. I'll show you to your rooms and you can unpack and wash up before dinner."

Rebecca liked the sound of that. Being around new people often overwhelmed her. She needed a moment of solitude and quiet to recoup so she could be in good form over dinner. She would have to see to Esther first, of course, help her unpack, but there should be at least a few minutes to spare for herself.

As it turned out, there was no spare room for her. The Fretzes were a larger family than her own, with fewer empty rooms. Esther was in the spare bedroom, a small room with a single, narrow bed. Simple, but comfortable enough. Meanwhile, Rebecca was sleeping on a small cot in with the two girls. Sandy seemed glad to have her there, while Ellen, the older girl, looked sullen, and wouldn't speak to her when Rebecca tried to make conversation.

"I'm sorry," Debbie told her as she showed her in. "It was this or the couch, and we thought this would give you a little more privacy, at least."

Rebecca smiled. "It's fine," she said. It would have to be. But she would be here for a month, that was all. And then she would go back to her own room in Esther's house, and back to her family and friends and her familiar life. If she wanted peace and quiet here, well, she only had to go outside. The Fretzes' farm looked huge compared to her own family's property, or even Esther's.

"Dinner will be ready in half an hour or so," Debbie told her and left her to unpack.

The girls had cleared out a drawer for her in the dresser and left some pegs empty for her to hang her dresses.

Afterward, Rebecca went to the room down the hall to make sure Esther had everything she needed. But Esther wasn't there. She found her, five minutes later, seated on a wooden rocking chair out on the enclosed porch, with the youngest boy, Ross, on her lap. He was sucking his thumb, and Esther was patting down his golden curls, as though she could tame them.

"Esther, wouldn't you rather sit inside by the warming stove?" Rebecca asked her, concerned. Esther was wrapped in her wool cloak and had a heavy-looking blanket spread out over her lap, but it was awfully cold, and she didn't want the woman to catch a chill. That would be no fun for either of them.

"I am sitting exactly where I mean to be sitting," Esther told her, her tone determined. "If I wanted to sit by the fire, that is where I would be."

Rebecca resisted the urge to roll her eyes or scowl at the woman and left Esther to her family bonding.

As she stepped outside for a short stroll about the place, part of her yearned to be with her own family. Christmas was always a good family gathering. They would all gather at

James's house, where his wife, Catherine, would arrange for everything. Rebecca, Iris, and *Mamm* would help.

There would be time for good conversation, and this year was the first year Rebecca should have spent with her new nephew. She sighed to herself—there was no point wishing for things she couldn't have. As *Mamm* had told her, she would have plenty more Christmas seasons, plenty more time to spend with her family, to hold her nephew and whatever other children might come into the family in the coming years. Esther only had now, and Rebecca should be glad for her, instead of pitying herself.

It was cold out, and Rebecca pulled her cloak a little tighter around shoulders. It must have been a dry winter in Baker's Corner so far, for the ground was hard under her shoes with no sign of rain nor even snow in the air. She passed a small orchard of bare apple and maybe pear trees and thought how lovely they would be in the summer, when the trees were green and laden with fruit.

Beyond the last row of trees was a narrow path, and beside that, there was the wood and wire fence that separated one property from another. She could see another house in the distance, painted white and pale green. It looked small from there, but surrounding it was a low-roofed barn and smaller outbuildings. Three—no, four, horses, wrapped up in their winter coats, grazed around those buildings.

Rebecca watched them for a while. Esther didn't have any

horses, but her own parents did. One was old now, but *Mamm* refused to sell her. She was part of the family, old Rosie was, a beautiful chestnut mare whose coat was now flecked with grey. These horses looked much younger, one barely out of colt-hood.

A man came around the side of the building then. Rebecca barely noticed him at first, not until he greeted the smallest of the four horses and fed her a handful of something from his pocket. He walked around the horse, toward another small building that might have been a chicken shed or a pig sty.

He was closer now, and Rebecca could see that he was well-built, broad-shouldered, and the hair curling out from under his hat was a dark blond. He caught sight of her then, and Rebecca felt her face warming despite the biting cold in the air. She hoped he couldn't see her blush from this distance and clung to that. But he merely smiled and waved, and Rebecca, after a moment, gave a small wave back, and turned back toward the house.

Chapter Four

Dinner was almost ready when Rebecca returned, and her mouth watered at the smell of cooking meat and vegetables. Esther was alone on her rocking chair now, and Rebecca helped her up and into the house. She settled her at the kitchen table and went to ask Debbie whether there was anything she could help with. Debbie insisted there wasn't, except perhaps to fill the twin metal jugs with milk for the table. Rebecca did as she was asked and then fetched the children to the table.

Once they were all seated, John led them in silent prayer. Rebecca bowed her head, thanking God for the safe trip and asking for help with tending to Esther in the coming days. When John cleared his throat signaling the end of the prayer, she helped pass the bowls of food around the table.

She had cut Esther's food up for her while in the kitchen, knowing that Esther often struggled, especially with meat, and now she poured a glass of milk for her, mopping up the few drops that escaped down the edge of the jug and onto the Fretzes' dining table.

Conversation flowed, but although Rebecca was asked questions about herself and her family, she felt strangely apart from it all. Unless she was spoken to directly, she stayed quiet, unsure of these people and of this place. She was almost glad to help Esther to the bathroom after dinner, glad for a chance to escape the overwhelming noise of a happy family when she was away from her own.

After dinner, there were chores to be done, but while John and Debbie tended to the children and the animals, Rebecca helped Esther. The old woman was tired from the journey, and it seemed that she too had found all the noise and commotion of this house taxing. She appeared asleep even before Rebecca closed the door to her room.

Instead of heading straight to bed herself, Rebecca headed down to the kitchen to help with the clean-up, but everything was done. The elder children sat at the table, chatting and drinking glasses of milk before bed.

Rebecca sat with them, and helped herself to another glass of milk, too. At her approach, the children fell quiet. That wouldn't do, Rebecca decided.

"You have a lovely home here," she said, hoping to initiate some conversation with them, even if it was only cursory.

Ellen shrugged, a gesture that Rebecca found jarring, almost rude.

"What's your home like?" Harry asked. "I've never been to Illinois."

Rebecca smiled. "Well, our house is a little bigger than this one, but our farm is smaller. We have seven sheep, three goats, two cows, and fifteen chickens."

"Do you have brothers and sisters?" Ellen wanted to know.

"One of each," Rebecca told her. "My brother is married now and has a baby of his own. My sister still lives at home, and I... Well, I live with your grandmother, so I can help her."

"Why?" Ellen asked, unblinking.

"Because she needs my help. It's our duty to help those in need," Rebecca told her. "And it's my job."

"Don't you want to get married?" Ellen asked, then, and Rebecca frowned at her forwardness. She'd had this conversation before, though, with her own grandmother and with her aunts, and, once, with Mary Joan.

"Well... *jah*. But that's not where my duty lies right now," she admitted. "If I find someone I like and want to marry, that might change things, but at the moment..."

"You're not courting anyone," Ellen said. "That's okay. I'm not, either."

Rebecca bit back a laugh. She certainly hoped thirteen-year-old Ellen wasn't courting boys just yet. She had a few more years until she needed to worry about that, Rebecca was sure. But something about the girl reminded her a little of Mary Joan. Ellen would surely turn out to be something of a busy body, Rebecca mused. Well, that was all right. Busy bodies were useful, in their own way.

"Tell me about your neighbors," Rebecca said, sipping her milk.

But it was Harry who answered.

"Well, the Farmers are on the left. They're old, and Mr. Farmer doesn't like us kids very much. But when he's out, Mrs. Farmer sometimes brings over pies and cobblers and tells us about the old days."

Rebecca smiled. They sounded a little like the Lapps, except Mr. Lapp was a jovial man, not in the slightest bit grumpy, and he'd loved them when they were children. They'd spent almost as much time at his house as they had their own.

"Behind us are the Schmuckers, they're a bit younger, more like your age I guess," Ellen said. "Bobby and Sandy play there sometimes because Thomas and Isabelle are the same ages."

"And you have the Rabers on the right," Harry told her.

This was what she'd wanted to know—who was the young man she'd waved to earlier? He'd seemed friendly, not to mention handsome... But no, Rebecca was only asking out of polite curiosity. And since she would be here for at least three weeks, it was good to know who the people around her were.

"I think I saw one of the Rabers this afternoon," Rebecca admitted. "A youngish man. Blond hair."

Ellen nodded. "That was probably Justin. Maybe his brother, Abram, but Abe lives down the hill now, so he's not there as much. Justin's usually around, though. He's nice enough."

"I don't like him," Harry said, frowning. "He never talks."

"Just because *you* have a big mouth," Ellen said, "doesn't mean everyone else does. Sometimes saying less is more."

Rebecca bit back a laugh at the expression on Harry's face. Surprise turned to nonchalance, and he took his glass into the kitchen to wash it up.

"I wouldn't get your hopes up about Justin though," Ellen said with a knowing look that made her seem older than her thirteen years. "He's courting Mary Ellen. I saw them together at the river last month. They're not official, but I think it's serious." She leaned in, and in half a whisper said, "I saw him kiss her. On the *mouth*."

Rebecca's eyes widened. She was less surprised to hear about the kiss than she was to hear Ellen say it. She really *was* a busy body.

Rebecca excused herself then, deciding it was more than time for bed. She went into the room, undressed quietly so as not to wake up Sandy, who was curled up in her bed, and lay down on the cot. The door opened minutes later and soon she could hear gentle snoring coming from Ellen's bed, too.

Rebecca was awake a while longer, though, thinking of home. Oh, how she wished she could be there now, in her own bed, close to the people who knew her, and whom she knew. She sighed. Talking of Justin Raber with Mary Ellen made her think about Daniel Shrock, his warm smile and green eyes. Three weeks here. Any chance she'd had with him was gone now, she knew. So much could happen in three weeks, and there were plenty of girls in her hometown who were interested in the new teacher.

The next morning, after breakfast, Rebecca found herself with enough time to take a walk. In someone else's house, there were few errands to perform. She made herself useful as she could, but her responsibilities were much less. Once Esther was washed and dressed and settled by the fire in the sitting room, Rebecca fastened her cloak and stepped outside. It was not too cold out today, a little warmer than the day previous, even, and she was glad for the fresh air. There were so many people bustling about in the house. Out here, she could think more freely and breathe in the fresh winter air. Just past the little orchard, she spread her arms out and turned, once, twice, three times, laughing. Oh, but it was good to be by herself for a moment. No one could see her now, no one could judge her.

But when she turned, she realized someone *could* see her. Justin Raber stood not far away at all, just across the fence, a pair of wire cutters in one hand and a length of wire in the other. His face reddened as their eyes met, and she felt her own cheeks heat up.

"*Gut* morning," she said, trying to act nonchalant.

He inclined his head to her. "It certainly seems it," he said, and she blushed again.

"Forgive me," she said. "I felt a little cooped up this morning."

Justin smiled. That was good—he must not think her crazy, then.

"I've felt much the same whenever I'm indoors," he admitted. "It's much better to be out under the sky, even if the sun is a little further away than I'd like."

Rebecca nodded in agreement. Silence stretched out for a moment. She wondered whether she should continue the conversation or make her excuses and walk away. Then he said, "I haven't seen you before."

There was a question there, although it hadn't been explicitly asked.

"I'm Rebecca Beck," she told him. "I'm from Land's Creek, in

Illinois. I'm accompanying Esther Fretz, John's mother. She's visiting her kin for Christmas."

"Oh," he said. "Well, I suppose that makes us neighbors for the month. I'm Justin Raber. Nice to meet you."

"Nice to meet you, too," Rebecca said, perhaps a trifle too earnestly. She liked Justin, she decided. She'd expected him to be a little more standoffish, from what Harry and Ellen had said about him last night, but he seemed conversational enough, polite and warm. His eyes were blue, she noticed, pale, wintery.

"Well," he said, a little awkwardly now. "This fence won't fix itself. I'd better get on with it."

"Of course," Rebecca said, trying not to feel disappointed that their meeting had ended so soon. "I'd best get back to the house at any rate."

He didn't reply to that, didn't say goodbye, and Rebecca turned and walked away with no further words between them. Odd, she thought, but oh well. People were strange sometimes. She knew she could be, that was for sure. She remembered his amused but slightly surprised expression as she'd slowed her spinning, and her cheeks warmed again.

How embarrassing.

Chapter Five

Justin had to take down and rebuild a whole panel of fencing. One of the cows had barged through it the week prior trying to get to her escaped calf. She'd pulled up three lengths of wire, cutting her forelegs in the process. He'd seen to the cow, smoothed anti-sceptic into the wounds, and she was healing well enough, although she wasn't letting her calf out of her sight.

The other cows seemed to be keeping an eye on the young cow as well. He was the only one so far, a frighteningly untimely calving that he hadn't expected—the poor thing had been small and fragile, and Justin thought for sure that he wouldn't survive more than a couple of days. But here he was, healthy and already causing havoc.

Justin looked over the fencing and thought to himself that it was a job well done. It should hold well enough, barring any more unfortunate mishaps with calves and their mothers.

He went back to the workshop to put away his tool bag and the remaining wire, and then headed up to the house to wash up. He was meeting Mary Ellen in a couple of hours, and it wouldn't do to be covered in dirt. He changed his clothes—the knees of his trousers were damp and earthy.

"Hello, son," his *mamm* said, laying her hand on his shoulder for just a second as he entered the kitchen.

He had prepared some food for himself and Mary Ellen and packed it away into a small hamper with plates, knives and forks for a winter picnic.

"Who was that you were talking to over the fence this morning?"

He smiled to himself—there was very little his mother didn't observe around here, and she liked to be in the know at all times.

"Rebecca Beck. She told me she's come over with John's mother for Christmas."

"Oh, from Illinois?"

"*Jah*, I believe so."

"Such a journey. Is she related, somehow?"

"I'm afraid I didn't ask," he told her. "From the way she

spoke, I would guess more of a family friend or something like that. She didn't speak about the Fretzes as though they knew each other well."

"So she's away from her family at Christmas?"

"I guess so," he said, fastening the hamper.

"Poor girl. That must be so unsettling. I'd hate to be without you all at Christmas."

"You're hatching a plan, aren't you, *Mamm?*" He knew her well enough to see she was thinking something.

"Well, of course, we must offer her some support, be friendly. She probably doesn't know anyone here except the Fretzes."

"Perhaps you should make a pie, take it over there and introduce yourself," Justin suggested. His mother had a good heart, but he knew part of her really just wanted all the gossip on the Beck girl in order to tell her friends. It wasn't often they had a newcomer in their midst. Within a few days, Rebecca would be the talk of the town. Poor Rebecca, he thought.

Then again, if he managed to pin Mary Ellen down and set a date, that might take some of the attention off the Beck girl. He was still hoping for a December wedding, even though it was already late November now. But there was still time. Perhaps today would be the day...

His spirits lifted a little at the thought, and he headed outside to put the hamper and a few quilts into the buggy. It wasn't quite the weather for a picnic, but theirs would be under cover, so he hoped it would be warm enough.

Mary Ellen was waiting at the end of her road for Justin when he approached. She still didn't like him to come to the house, although he was on good terms with both her parents, and although their relationship still largely a secret, her father knew about it and approved. But Justin honored Mary Ellen's wishes; there was no reason not to, after all. He would be part of her family soon enough, once they were married.

Mary Ellen slipped her arm through his, and he urged the gray mare leading the buggy into motion. It was a quiet day, no one on the road, and Mary Ellen laughed with him as he talked about his mother's not-so-subtle plans for the Beck girl.

"Perhaps *I* should go and visit her," Mary Ellen said. "I could use a new friend, and this town is awfully dull at times. Perhaps a mysterious girlfriend from Illinois could shake things up a little."

Justin rolled his eyes. Truly, she was as bad as his mother.

He parked the buggy down a dirt road, and they walked the rest of the way across the empty field to the old barn. The barn had once belonged to Herb Tipp, but the old man had passed away earlier in the year, and the land had still yet to be sold. Justin laid out quilts over hay bales and set down the hamper.

"Oh, how sweet," Mary Ellen exclaimed. "Although you *do* realize it's winter, don't you, Justin? Picnics are generally more appropriate for the summer months."

"Well, *jah,* but I thought since we're inside..." He frowned. Maybe he *had* been foolish. What was he thinking? A picnic in the middle of winter? Honestly. He really was hopeless, as Mary Ellen so often told him.

"Oh, don't be cross," she said then, brushing his upper sleeve with her hand. She had such soft hands, did Mary Ellen. He had liked the feel of them on his face, that one time she'd touched his cheeks. "If it's cold, well then, we'll just have to warm each other up."

Justin blushed, and Mary Ellen laughed. She was the most forward girl Justin had ever met, but he rather liked it.

They sat close together, and Mary Ellen wrapped her arm around his shoulders, reaching up to stroke his hair. The feel of her hand through his curls was delicious, and as her fingers stroked down the back of his neck, he shivered, his face heating. He wriggled away from her touch, just a little, the sensation overwhelming. "Shall we eat?" he asked, and Mary Ellen agreed they should.

So they ate—boiled eggs, cold meats, sandwiches and dried fruit. By the time they were done, he was fully satisfied. Mary

Ellen pushed aside her plate and plopped back on the quilt. She sighed, and there was something a little sad in it, he fancied.

"Mary Ellen," he started, and she laughed at the serious note in his voice. Mary Ellen so rarely liked to be serious. It made things... difficult. He tried again, "What do you think about Tuesday, December fifteenth?" he asked.

"It's a day," she said, "more or less like any other. Why?"

"I mean, what do you think about it for our wedding?"

She sighed again. "Why the rush?" she asked. "Wouldn't you rather wait until next year sometime? A summer wedding would be much nicer, don't you think?"

"We've been secretly engaged for months now," he reminded her. "That's hardly rushing. I don't want to wait any longer. I love you, Mary Ellen, and I want to marry you. Don't you want to marry me?"

She clutched his arm then, her grip firm. He turned to look down at her, but she was staring up at the roof. "Of course, I do. I'm just not sure I want all the fuss so close to Christmas. Are you sure you wouldn't rather wait?"

"I *have* waited. And I *will* wait, if that's what you truly want, but you must know how I feel about you. I just want to know that you feel the same."

She sighed for the third time. "Justin..." she began, and then she sat up. She leaned over him, a strand of blonde hair falling out from under her *kapp*, and she kissed him. It was a gentle thing, a brief touch of their lips, the way she'd kissed him before, but there was more of a promise in that kiss now.

"All right then," she declared. "Let's get married. December fifteenth it is. I suppose I'm really only delaying the inevitable, aren't I?"

The inevitable? he thought. What a way to put it.

"What does it matter if it's December or May?" she said, her words coming slower now. "It's the same thing, in the end, and if sooner makes you happy... Well, dear Justin, I *do* want to make you happy." Her lips curved at that, and Justin felt himself grow warm at the strange, sensual undertone in her voice.

"You *do* make me happy," he admitted, pulling her close. She was warm against him, and he brushed her cheek, savoring the feel of her smooth, soft skin. They rubbed noses, and both of them laughed. Amusement sparkled in Mary Ellen's eyes, where before they had seemed sad, and he was relieved to see the change. He didn't like it when Mary Ellen was sad. Sometimes, he wondered if she even wanted to get married at all, but now...

"I'll tell *Mamm* and *Dat* tonight," he decided. "Perhaps we can be published this Sunday."

She nodded slowly, still smiling, and pulled away from him, sitting back up. "All right then," she said. "Sunday it is."

He drove her home then, but she was silent throughout the journey, no doubt lost in thought, thinking of all the planning she would have to do for the wedding. He knew girls often thought of their wedding day long before it ever came about, even as children. It would be simple enough, but knowing Mary Ellen, she would want *something* a little unique about it.

He helped Mary Ellen down from the buggy and kissed her on the cheek, a quiet farewell for now. She turned and walked up the road, and he watched her for just a moment before climbing back up onto the buggy.

His mare took him down the road and right toward his family's farm. Not far from home, he spotted a lone figure walking, a young lady. She turned at the sound of the buggy and smiled. It was Rebecca Beck. He slowed the horse and bade Miss Beck a good day.

"Aren't you chilled out walking?" he asked.

"Oh, not really, I'm just out for a stroll. I have a lot more free time here than I usually do at home, so I thought I'd learn to enjoy it."

She really was rather pretty, he thought, with a fine smattering of freckles over high cheekbones. Of course, she wasn't quite as beautiful as Mary Ellen. But he was sure she would be well-received around here. She *did* have that element of mystery going for her, being from out of town.

"Can I offer you a lift?" he asked, but she shook her head.

"It's not too far," she said, "and I'm very much enjoying the fresh air. But thank you."

He tipped his hat to her and went on his way.

Chapter Six

Esther stared at Rebecca as she walked into the Fretzes' sitting room. She was in the chair closest to the warming stove, with a thick quilt over her knees.

"Where on earth have you been?" Esther asked her.

Rebecca had been gone little under an hour, but she was not surprised to find Esther in a bad mood. If it were up to Esther, Rebecca would be in at least two or three places at once, all of them catering to Esther's needs.

"I took a short walk around the property and down along the road," she said, keeping her tone pleasant. "Perhaps you should come with me next time. We could just go for a little wander, not too far."

Esther's scowl deepened. "I needed you here," she told

Rebecca. "I can't find my reading glasses, and I didn't want to bother my grand-*kinner*. Where did you put them?"

"On your night table," Rebecca told her, "Where you always keep them."

Esther was quiet a moment, staring at her with judgement in her eyes. Rebecca felt very small under Esther's cool gaze.

"Well?" Esther said then, her tone harsh. "What are you waiting for? Go and get them."

Rebecca bit her lip, and then turned and marched from the room. She'd been so excited the day she'd gotten this job, but now... Of course, she'd known then that it wouldn't be easy— she'd known Esther had a bad temper and a biting tongue, but somehow, she'd thought it would be different, that Esther would be more... well, grateful, she supposed.

She laughed a little at herself, then, at how foolish she'd been to think that. Why would Esther be grateful, when her body and even her mind were failing her? Rebecca knew that Esther resented having to rely on someone else for so many things. If she were in Esther's place, she might resent that too. But to take it out on the person who was trying to help her? *Ach*, it would be so nice if she and Esther could be friends. Instead, Rebecca found herself more and more at odds with the woman.

She blinked back tears and told herself not to be so silly. She wasn't a child.

She opened the door to Esther's room and walked across to the nightstand. There, beside the small gas lamp, were Esther's reading glasses. Rebecca picked them up and headed back down the stairs to the sitting room. When she got there, Esther took the glasses from her without a word of thanks.

Instead, she said, "Finally!" before picking up her book and beginning to read. Rebecca was dismissed.

Holding her breath, teeth biting into her lower lip, Rebecca left the room and the old woman behind her.

Dearest Gott, give me strength, Rebecca prayed silently. *Give me patience. I know Esther needs me, but couldn't you make it a little easier on both of us?*

But of course, that wasn't *Gott's* role. Life was full of trials. Esther had taught Rebecca that much over the last year. All she could hope for was the grace to endure them.

Rebecca offered to check on the hens, never mind that she'd only just been outside no more than half an hour ago—but it was an excuse to get away for a moment or two. She hummed to herself as she walked, taking a look in the chicken coops to see if there were any eggs to collect. She peeked in boxes and in narrow spaces where the hens might lay, but she found nothing. Any eggs must have been collected that morning.

A small brown hen with patches of feathers missing from her back and wings clucked at Rebecca's feet. Not overly fond of hens, Rebecca surprised herself by stooping to pick her up.

The hen was calm and placid in her arms, and as Rebecca stroked a finger over her chest, the hen clucked quiet sounds.

Rebecca would have to write to her mother later and ask how Esther's hens were doing under the neighbor's care. Esther would likely enjoy hearing about them.

She let the hen back down and wandered through the now barren orchard as if drawn by some invisible force, toward the fence that separated the Fretzes' property from the Rabers'. She couldn't fool herself as to why she was walking this way. She wanted to talk to Justin. He was so pleasant.

But Justin wasn't there. Of course, he wasn't, she thought to herself. Their last encounters here had been mere chance. It wasn't as though Justin stood by this fence all day every day waiting for her to come along. She rolled her eyes at herself and turned to go back inside.

She had barely climbed the two steps up to the porch when someone called out behind her. She turned to see an unfamiliar woman walking up the driveway, a wicker basket hanging from one arm.

The woman smiled at her as she approached. "Why, you must be Rebecca Beck," she said. "I'm Hope Raber. I live just next door. I believe you've already met my youngest son, Justin?"

Rebecca nodded. "It's a pleasure to meet you," she said. "Are you here to see Debbie?"

"Partly," Hope admitted. "But I also thought I should come

and introduce myself to you. You're here for Christmas, I believe?"

Rebecca nodded.

"Well then, that's no time to be among strangers. We must make you an honorary member of our community here, so to speak."

Rebecca smiled at that. Hope's manner was warm and welcoming. It was exactly what Rebecca needed right then.

"Would you like to come in?" she asked, and Hope followed her into the house.

Rebecca checked in on Esther, who had fallen asleep in her chair, her book open on her blanketed lap, her reading glasses sliding down her nose. Rebecca removed the glasses and the book and set them on the table beside Esther's chair for safekeeping, and then followed Hope into the kitchen, where she had already seated herself at the kitchen table.

Rebecca made tea, and offered cookies, but Hope declined the latter. "I've brought a pie," Hope told her. "I know, I know. We're all baking up a storm right now, but I had some time on my hands and I thought you all might enjoy it."

Rebecca smiled and thanked her. It really was very thoughtful.

"Mrs. Raber," Sandy's voice piped up from the doorway. The little girl was a sight—her apron smudged and dirty, her feet bare, and her gold curls escaping from under her *kapp*.

Rebecca went to her, adjusting her *kapp* for her. That was a little better.

"What have you been doing?" Rebecca asked her.

"Digging," she said, proudly.

"Digging?" Hope said, sounding surprised. "But the ground's half frozen."

"*Nee,* it ain't," Sandy said. "Me and Bobby put some potatoes in. *Dat* says it's way too early, but I think they'll grow."

Rebecca smiled to herself. One day, Sandy would be an expert farmer.

"Would you like a slice of pie?" Rebecca asked her. "Mrs. Raber's made it special."

Sandy's eyes went wide. "Can I?"

Rebecca unwrapped the pie and cut slices for all three of them, making sure Sandy's was only a thin slice—she was such a small girl, after all.

After she'd eaten the pie, Sandy excused herself and went upstairs, hopefully to change but more than likely to play with her dolls. Hope and Rebecca chatted awhile, and it was nice.

"Well now, I *am* surprised to hear John's mother has come to visit," Hope said. "We've lived next door for... oh, going on sixteen years now, and she's not been here to see him in all that time. Although I know John dotes on her in his own way.

He did tell my husband, Adam that he hoped she would come this year, but he didn't think it was very likely."

"Esther is... well, she's a little set in her ways," Rebecca admitted. "But I know she dotes on John, too. She always looks forward to his letters, so I think it's wonderful *gut* that she's come all this way to see him."

"I don't doubt it," Hope said warmly. "Kin is so important, especially at this time of year."

Rebecca tried not to show the ache those words caused. She missed her family, her friends, and her community. She wished she could be with them right now and still be able to take care of Esther.

"Oh, I'm sorry, dear, mentioning kin like that," Hope said, and Rebecca knew her attempts at stoicism had failed. "You must be missing your relatives about now."

She bit her lip and nodded. "It's all right, though," she said. "It's important for me to be here right now. I know I'll see them soon enough, and we'll have our get-together then."

"You have a very positive outlook," Hope said, sounding approving. "I think you must be a very practical young woman."

Rebecca liked the way she said 'young woman' and not 'girl'. She hadn't felt like a girl for a long time, certainly not since she'd started working for Esther.

"I do try to be practical," Rebecca told her, and Hope smiled.

Hope made her excuses then, and left, only meeting Debbie on her way out, who had just come up from the basement. They chatted for a while, and Rebecca left them to it. When she checked on Esther, the old woman was still asleep, and Rebecca breathed a sigh of relief.

Chapter Seven

Justin was on his way out the door when his mother told him he'd be giving Rebecca Beck a lift into town. He knew he couldn't refuse, and neither did he want to, although his mother seemed to think he needed persuading, because she did rather go on about how Rebecca was new to town and wouldn't know the way, and how it was such a long walk in this cold weather, and didn't it look like it might rain or perhaps snow?

So, Justin drove the buggy up the Fretzes' driveway and knocked on the door. Rebecca was already dressed in her cloak, her shopping basket hanging from her arm.

"Thank you so much for this," she told him. "It's really very kind of you."

He waved her thanks away. It was no trouble.

"Do you have any errands to run?" Rebecca asked him once she was seated in the front seat of the buggy.

"A few," he said. In fact, he was meeting Mary Ellen, but he wanted to keep that private. And it wasn't a lie exactly—he *did* have errands to run as well.

He was looking forward to seeing his fiancée. It had been a few days since they'd decided on a date for the wedding, and they needed to discuss matters further. Justin had already gone to the bishop to ask whether they could be published at such short notice. Thankfully, the bishop had agreed that they could, although they would have to be published alone rather than in a group of other betrothed couples. Everyone else, the bishop had told him, was far more organized and all the December weddings had been announced already. Theirs would be a week later than everyone else, he'd said.

Justin didn't mind that. All he could think about was that he'd soon be married to Mary Ellen.

His good mood must have shown on his face, because Rebecca commented, "Looks like you're right happy this day."

"Well, it's a beautiful day," Justin said, grinning.

Rebecca looked up at the sky skeptically. "It looks a bit overcast." She laughed.

He joined her. "Well, that's one perspective," he replied. "But you can also look at the fact that it's *not raining yet*."

Rebecca smiled at that. Her face lit up beautifully when she smiled, he noted. He dropped her off in the center of town, and then went on his way toward the park where he was due to meet Mary Ellen.

Mary Ellen had a part-time job in the town, working for an older Mennonite couple in their shop selling artisan soaps and candles and various other knickknacks. She was due to finish at two o'clock today, and the clock in the town square told him it was five minutes to the hour.

He parked the buggy at the side of the quiet path that cut through the park, used by walkers, cyclists and joggers, but never cars, and took a seat on the wooden bench under the pagoda where they had often met. The town clock rang out the hour, and Justin waited impatiently.

Ten minutes passed, then twenty. He frowned to himself. Where on earth was she? He supposed she might be finishing work late, perhaps there was a late lunch rush or something...

He waited.

The first drops of rain began to fall, a light patter against the pagoda roof. He thought of the horses and hoped Mary Ellen had her umbrella with her. She would get wet, walking in this. The town clock chimed three times. Mary Ellen was an hour late.

That was it, he decided. Whatever had happened to her, he couldn't sit around here any longer. The horse was whickering, growing restless. He would drive by Mary Ellen's work and see if she was still there.

She wasn't. The woman who ran the shop, Mrs. Olsen, told him she'd left early that afternoon, and had said she errands to run. She hadn't said a word about meeting anyone.

Worry flickered through him. What had happened to her? Although... It wasn't the first time she had done this, was it? When they'd first started courting, Mary Ellen had been so unreliable that Justin had almost called things off. The last few months, however, she'd been better, and had only been late a handful of times. Had she simply forgotten him? Did she have other things on her mind?

He sighed to himself, feeling disappointed and annoyed, and yes, more than a little worried now. Two hours had passed, he realized as the clock rang out four times. He had said he would take Rebecca home again at four, and so that was it for his date with Mary Ellen.

He met Rebecca at the same spot where he'd dropped her off. She was already waiting for him, the hood of her cloak drawn to protect herself from the light smattering of rain.

"I told you it was overcast," she said, smiling.

"So you did," he replied. "Did you savor the hour of dry weather?"

"It was glorious," she told him. "So good I wish I could turn back time and enjoy it all over again. I'm afraid I've gotten rather wet."

He glanced across at her. "I'm sorry about that," he told her.

"It's all right. I don't think I'll catch a chill."

He laughed. "I hope not. But, if you mean a cold or the flu, those things pass person to person you know." He faked a loud, forceful sneeze, and Rebecca stared at him for a second, before bursting into peals of laughter.

He smiled. His afternoon might not have been what he'd hoped for, but he supposed it wasn't *all* bad.

Justin dropped Rebecca off at the end of the road. It had stopped raining, and the sun was peeking out from behind the clouds. Rebecca had insisted that she walk the rest of the way. Her basket of purchases wasn't at all heavy, she'd assured him.

The Gropps lived a few miles away, on a farm half the size of his own family's. They kept few animals. Mr. Gropp was a woodworker, and there was a small stand of pines at the back of the house that made the place look rather ominous.

Mary Ellen was the youngest of four girls, and the Gropps had no sons. She was the only one still unmarried, a fact she'd often commented on when they had first started courting. Justin had taken that as something of a hint, but he wondered now whether it had been more a matter of pride for her. But no, that was silly. She *was* marrying him. Today was nothing but a misunderstanding, he was sure.

He knocked on the door, and Mrs. Gropp answered with a warm smile. Justin got along well with Mary Ellen's parents, always had. He'd worked a little for them before he and Mary Ellen began courting, helping out on their place when Mr. Gropp had fallen ill the previous summer.

Mrs. Gropp gave him a knowing look when he inquired after Mary Ellen. She was in, it turned out, and had barely gotten home. Mrs. Gropp asked him to wait in the kitchen and made him a cup of tea. Mary Ellen had gotten caught in the rain, she said, and needed to change out of her wet clothes.

Justin held the cup of tea in both hands, warming himself. It was a while before Mary Ellen came down to see him, looking both surprised and sheepish.

"Justin," she said, a little breathlessly. "Oh, Justin, I'm so sorry. I completely forgot we were meant to meet today. Work was so busy, and all I could think was how much I wanted to get out of there and get home, but then my bike had a puncture, and... Well, I *am* sorry. I do hope you were waiting somewhere dry."

"Thankfully, I was," he said. Her excuse had done little to lessen his irritation with her. But if he was going to marry her, he needed to get used to it. Honestly, Rebecca had been where she was supposed to be, and on time, too. Why couldn't Mary Ellen be like that?

"I spoke to the bishop," he said, deciding to get down to business. He couldn't stay long, and there were important things to discuss. "He says it's fine for us to be published next Sunday, and our wedding will be announced for the fifteenth."

Mary Ellen smiled a small, tight smile. "Sounds fine," she said.

"Is it all right?" he asked, feeling the need to reassure himself. She didn't seem as enthusiastic as he'd hoped, although he supposed his own manner in discussing it was rather brusque. This wasn't how he'd wanted today to be.

"*Jah,* I'm sure," she said. "It's just... well, there's so much to think about, isn't there? I suppose can get a wedding dress made that quickly. I know *Mamm* and even *Mammi* will help me.

Justin smiled. There, Mary Ellen was getting into it now. He breathed a sigh of relief. Everything was just as it should be.

Chapter Eight

Rebecca busied herself in the kitchen that afternoon, helping Debbie and Ellen with the Christmas baking. The other children helped too, albeit with varying degrees of effort. Harry wandered in and out, mostly eating the cookie mix, while Bobby watched the goings-on quietly, occasionally adding a few decorative touches. Sandy and Ross sat on the floor, banging wooden spoons together and generally making a racket.

Esther had excused herself to the sitting room once the children came in. The noise was too much for her, Rebecca thought. She wasn't used to it, and her hearing wasn't the best —she'd once told Rebecca that too much noise blurred together and got confusing. For a while, though, she'd sat at the table and instructed Debbie and Rebecca on the right way to make a Christmas cake. Debbie had learned a different recipe, so they'd decided to make two cakes. That way everyone was happy.

Rebecca's thoughts drifted as she rolled out the cookie dough, occasionally sprinkling a little extra flour over the counter to make sure it didn't stick to the surface. She kept thinking about Justin, and his smile...

When he'd picked her up that afternoon to take her home, though, he'd seemed somehow sad. Yes, they'd joked, but there had been worry in his eyes. She hoped he was all right. Perhaps he just didn't like the weather, although they'd joked about it enough. It was nice to spend time with someone who made her laugh, she thought. She missed her friends back home but being with Justin made her feel more content.

"*Ach!*" Debbie said, suddenly. "We're out of apple spice. How silly of me. I should have remembered to ask you to get some while you were in town, Rebecca."

"I'm sure we can make do..." Rebecca started.

"*Nee, nee.* I'll just have to pop next door and see if Hope has any. I'm sure she won't mind. Would you watch the children for me?"

Rebecca told her that of course she would, and Debbie promised she would only be a few minutes. It was probably closer to an hour later when Debbie returned, however, and she had a sly smile on her face that promised news.

"You'll never guess," she said, more to her elder children than to Rebecca. Still, Rebecca was intrigued.

"Justin is going to marry Mary Ellen," she exclaimed. "Hope tells me they'll be published on Sunday. I don't think she meant to say it aloud, but goodness that woman can't keep anything to herself for long."

Something twisted inside Rebecca's chest. She turned her attention to the dough in front of her, working it with the heavy roller. She'd known Justin and Mary Ellen were courting. Ellen had told her as much. Why was she so disappointed? It wasn't as though she'd ever had a chance with Justin. Why, they were just friends, and wasn't that wonderful to have a friend in Baker's Corner?

In a few weeks, Rebecca would be heading back to Land's Creek with Esther, anyway.

"I *told* you," Ellen said to Harry, who merely shrugged.

"And *I* told *you*, I don't care," Harry said, although his tone was jovial. "I mean, it's nice for them and all, but I don't see how it's any of our business."

"Except that we'll all be attending the wedding service," Debbie reminded him.

Harry frowned. "Ugh," he said, but Debbie didn't reprimand him.

"I *love* weddings," Ellen said gleefully, more to Rebecca now. "Don't you?"

"They're lovely," Rebecca said, her tone flat. She did like weddings, it was true, but for some reason she couldn't feel quite so happy about this one. She'd never met Mary Ellen, although she supposed she should be pleased for Justin. She wanted him to be happy, even though she didn't know him well or for very long.

She was almost grateful when Esther called her away from the hustle and bustle of the kitchen. Perhaps Esther's company wasn't quite as sweet, but at least it meant she could escape the wedding discussion.

Rebecca went to bed that night feeling strange. Something wasn't quite right. Perhaps it was just homesickness, she thought. Everything would be well again once she was home.

Rebecca wasn't sure what awoke her in the middle of the night. A thump or a thud, perhaps? But then she heard someone cry out, and instinct took over. She jumped out of her cot and hurried from the girls' room and into Esther's room next door. She fumbled to get the lamp lit.

Esther lay on the floor in the middle of the small room, one arm under her head. She wasn't moving, and for a moment

Rebecca's breath caught in her throat. And then, Esther's voice screeched out, "Are you going to help me or not?"

Rebecca stifled a laugh—Esther was all right. She hurried across to her, helping to ease her up to a sitting position. She assessed the damage—Esther's right shoulder was sore, but she seemed otherwise unharmed. Thank the good Lord.

Rebecca half-lifted Esther to her feet and helped her to the bed, where the old woman waved her aside. They were both silent a moment.

"Would you like some water?" Rebecca asked.

Esther scowled at her but nodded.

When Rebecca returned with the water, Esther thanked her. She actually thanked her. Rebecca bit her lip, worried the old woman might have bumped her head in the fall.

"I'll sleep in here tonight," she said, "Make sure everything's all right."

"Oh, wonderful, so now I have to listen to you snoring all night," Esther muttered, but she didn't argue. They both knew that it would be the other way around—Esther was the one who snored.

She fetched her cot from the girls' room as quietly as possible and set herself up near the door in Esther's room. Esther was already back under her quilts, although she was not asleep.

"Is there anything else you need?" Rebecca asked.

"A *gut* night's sleep, is what I need," Esther said. "Don't fuss, it's unbecoming."

It's my job, Rebecca thought. *I literally get paid to fuss.* But now wasn't the time for needless arguments, and so, she settled down to sleep.

Chapter Nine

Justin tried not to breathe in the fragrant floral scents of the shop as he stood by the back door, waiting for Mary Ellen to finish serving her customer. The smell of the shop was overwhelming to him, but it suited Mary Ellen well enough. She too, felt a little overwhelming to him at times. As the customer exited the shop, Mary Ellen walked over to the front door and flipped the sign around. The shop was now closed, at least for an hour, at any rate.

Mary Ellen was working late today, it being a Saturday, and Justin had decided it was the perfect time to surprise her with lunch. However, Mary Ellen hadn't looked overly pleased. Instead, she'd been confused, and then a little curt. But sometimes, that was just Mary Ellen; Justin wondered if he would ever figure her out.

She squeezed his hand in greeting, and then led him through to the little room in the back where they could sit and eat.

"You didn't have to do this," she said for the fourth or fifth time. "It's lovely of you, but you didn't need to come out of your way, not for me."

"Mary Ellen," Justin replied, "I would do anything for you. Do you really think a short buggy ride into town is overdoing it?"

She smiled at that. "You really are a nice man."

Justin felt his cheeks heat up a little, but he smiled. He decided to busy himself unpacking the lunch his mother had prepared—half a cold vegetable pie, bread, cheese, and sugared apples for dessert. It was rather simple, but Mary Ellen's face lit up.

"This looks delicious," she declared, then admitted, "I'm afraid I was in rather a rush this morning, so I completely forgot to bring lunch. I was going to have toast."

"Then I'm glad I'm here," Justin said. "We can't have you eating toast for lunch. That won't do at all. Here you go." He cut off a slice of the vegetable pie and placed it onto a small plate. He pushed it across the little table toward her.

"Thank you," Mary Ellen said and began to eat.

For a moment, Justin watched her. She really was very beautiful, he thought. If only he knew what was going on in her thoughts. For someone who talked so much, she gave away very little. She glanced up, and her gaze caught his. She'd caught him watching, and he ducked his head a little, his face heating up. She said nothing about it, however, and for a while they ate in silence.

"It's only a few days now," Justin said.

Mary Ellen put down her fork and looked at him. "A few days?" she asked.

Justin frowned. How had she forgotten? "Until we're published," he reminded her.

"*Jah.*" Her voice was small and quiet, and she seemed lost in thought for a moment, until, "I hadn't forgotten if that's what you're thinking. I just... I keep getting confused lately."

"Confused?" Justin asked. "What do you mean?" Perhaps the shop had been too busy that morning. There was a lot going on, he supposed. Mary Ellen might be overwhelmed by it all. But she should be excited, too. She didn't *seem* excited, though.

"It's going to be wonderful *gut*," Justin told her, trying to cheer her up. "We'll have our special meal together, and when we're finished, everyone will know about us, and it... well, it will be all official and everything. Everyone will be so pleased for us."

"Of course, they will," Mary Ellen said. "I just... Everyone will fuss so."

"You deserved to be fussed over. This will be our moment. Enjoy it."

She nodded, distant. Justin frowned. What could he say to make her feel better about this?

"You do ... want to marry me, don't you?" he asked, again feeling uncertainty surge through him.

"Of course," she told him then, her gaze not quite meeting his. "There is no one in the district I would rather marry. You've been so *gut* to me." Her gaze met his then, and he knew she meant it.

Justin smiled and nodded.

After lunch with Mary Ellen, Justin ran a few errands his mother had asked him to do, purchasing feed for both their animals and the Fretzes', whose buggy had a damaged wheel that they hadn't yet found the time to fix. Justin would have taken a look at it, but he hadn't found the time lately either. December was always a busy month, and on top of that, he was due to be married. There was so much to think about, that he'd almost completely forgotten about the Fretzes' buggy.

He dropped the feed off at the Fretzes', storing it neatly in their barn for them before knocking to let them know it was there.

Rebecca answered the door. Debbie was over at the Farmers' next door, and John was mending a fence at the back of the property, along with his two eldest sons. Rebecca had been left home with the other three children and the elder Mrs. Fretz. Rebecca looked tired, as though she hadn't slept all that well, although it would have been impolite for him to comment on it.

"I hear congratulations are in order," Rebecca said.

Justin frowned. "How do you know about that?"

Rebecca worried her lower lip with her teeth. "Sorry," she said. "I shouldn't have let on. But... well, *jah*, we know already I'm afraid."

"I'll bet that was my *mamm's* doing," he muttered. He'd have to have words with her when he got home, not that it would do much good, of course.

"I couldn't possibly say," Rebecca said, and Justin laughed. "But really, I am glad for you. It's such a wonderful thing."

"It is, isn't it?" Justin said. Somehow, Rebecca was managing to show more enthusiasm for his wedding than his fiancée was.

"Will it be soon?" Rebecca asked. "It would be nice to attend. If I'm welcome, that is."

"Of course, you're welcome. You're my very *gut* neighbor for the month, and you're an honorary part of our community now. You will be coming to preaching service on Sunday, I take it?"

Rebecca nodded. "Of course. I missed my first Sunday here because we'd only just arrived, and Esther was too tired. Although, I don't suppose I'll see you there."

Justin shook his head. "I'm afraid not. I'll be with my fiancée eating the traditional meal, but I'm sure we'll catch up over the fence before the wedding."

Rebecca smiled at that. She was really quite pretty, he thought, and then scolded himself. He shouldn't be thinking that way. He was betrothed now, and Rebecca was merely a neighbor, perhaps a friend, but nothing more.

Although of course, he supposed he could be objective... She really *was* quite good-looking. Not that it was important. More important was Rebecca's manner. Matter-of-fact, but good-humored. She knew her duties and strove to do them well. She took care of those who needed it. He couldn't imagine Mary Ellen caring for someone in their old age, although he supposed that was a little unfair of him. She might surprise him. Mary Ellen was always surprising him, one way or another, albeit not always in a positive manner...

He'd lingered on this porch too long, he decided, and bid Rebecca good day. Tomorrow, he would be published. He'd never thought this day would come. He'd thought, really, that he'd be a little more excited. Instead, his nerves worried his stomach and doubt pulled at his mind. Perfectly normal, he told himself, understanding now how Mary Ellen might be feeling. Natural to be nervous, to have a few last-minute doubts. It was a big thing, perhaps the most important moment of his life. It would be strange *not* to be nervous, he decided.

So, it was all right, he and Mary Ellen could be nervous together.

Chapter Ten

Justin awoke early that morning. He hadn't slept well. It was Sunday, the day his and Mary Ellen's wedding was to be published at the church. Once that was done, there would be no going back, he realized. *Have I made a mistake?* he wondered, vaguely, as he buttoned his shirt and headed down to the kitchen for breakfast. Was Mary Ellen really the one for him?

He shook his head in frustration. Of course, Mary Ellen was the one for him. They had fun together, didn't they? She made him laugh, and he couldn't deny he liked that in a woman. She had her weak points, but didn't everyone? He certainly did.

But did she even like him? He'd never been sure of that. "She's marrying me, isn't she?" he said out loud, the words sounding strange in the empty room.

He was just ready to have a cup of tea when a knock sounded at the door. It was loud, heavy, the sound of someone thumping their fist hard against the wood.

He hurried to the door and opened it to find Abram Gropp standing on the porch, his fist raised to knock again.

"Oh," Justin said, surprised. "*Gut* morning."

But Abram Gropp's face looked as though there was nothing good about this particular morning at all. "Is Mary Ellen here?" he demanded.

Justin frowned. "*Nee*," he answered, wondering why on earth Mr. Gropp thought she'd be here so early in the morning. He was due to head over to their house soon.

Abram's shoulders slumped. "I'm afraid we can't find her this morning," he said. "I thought she might be here, but..."

"Maybe she went out for a morning walk?" Justin suggested, threading his fingers together in front of him and then forcing himself to relax them by his sides. "She'll have a lot on her mind right now."

"*Jah,* I know, but... Well, she's supposed to be cooking with her mother this morning. They were getting up early. You're probably right, of course, but her mother does like to worry, so I told her I'd come and ask." None of the concern had left his face, however, and that made Justin only more nervous.

"Why don't we give her an hour?" Justin suggested. "If she's not back by then, we'll look for her."

Abram nodded.

"I'll be by in an hour," Justin told him, and closed the door as Abram walked down the steps and away from the house.

There was no reason to worry, Justin told himself. Was there?

Rebecca had ridden to church in the neighbor's buggy to the south—the Fretzes' own had been out of commission for a week now. She'd gone with the younger children and Debbie, while John, Esther, Harry and Ellen had ridden in with the Farmers.

Rebecca hesitated a moment before taking her seat in the unmarried women's section of the room. She knew very few people here, and that felt strange. In Land's Creek, she would always sit with Mary Joan, but here in Baker's Corner, she was alone.

Still, she knew a few people, she supposed—the Fretzes, the Farmers, the Schmucker children, and oh, there were the Rabers now, walking in the door. She smiled at Hope, but she seemed preoccupied and didn't meet Rebecca's gaze. *Well*, Rebecca thought, deciding not to take it personally; it was the day of her son's publication—she'd certainly have other things on her mind.

But the publication never came. Rebecca prayed and sang hymns, all the while awaiting the announcement, the thought of it ticking over in the back of her head, but the service ended, and nothing was said about Justin and Mary Ellen. Rebecca frowned. She looked over at the Rabers, but their expressions gave nothing away.

Something must be wrong, Rebecca thought as she stood to leave. What on earth had happened? She hoped Justin was all right.

Don't be silly, she told herself. *Would the Rabers be here if something was wrong with Justin? Nee, they wouldn't. They would be with him.*

So, then what? Had he and Mary Ellen broken off their engagement? Surely not at this short notice. And from what Ellen had told her, she'd have thought Justin was besotted with Mary Ellen.

The thought crossed her mind then that she should go to him, make sure he really *was* all right, maybe comfort him or bring him a pie or *something*. But of course, that was out of the question. Whatever had happened, it was none of her business.

"*Justin* won't have broken it off," Debbie said later, as they were walking up the driveway toward the house. "*Nee*, he's always been very true to his word. If there was anything of that sort going on, it'll be down to Mary Ellen, you mark my words."

"Will he be all right, do you think?" Rebecca asked. "I can't imagine how I'd feel if something like that happened to me."

Rebecca's arm was looped through Esther's, and she could feel the old woman looking at her. "Don't you go thinking you can get your foot in that door," Esther said, low enough so no one else could hear. "You're an Illinois girl."

Rebecca whipped her gaze around to stare at Esther. How could she say something like that, even *think* something like that?

To the group, Esther said, loudly, "You lot are twittering like a flock of swallows. We've no idea what's happened, so perhaps we should wait for the facts, first."

Now *that* was more sensible, Rebecca thought begrudgingly. Esther was right. They were gossiping and assuming the worst. Perhaps Justin and Mary Ellen had only delayed the wedding.

Yes, that was probably all it was.

Justin slumped in the wicker chair on the porch, barely feeling the cold. They had looked everywhere for Mary Ellen, but she was nowhere to be found.

I know you won't want to hear it, his father had said, *but I don't think you should be published today. Not until she turns up.*

Justin had agreed. It was likely that Mary Ellen would show up soon enough, but until she did, there was no way he was taking that risk. She should be in her family's kitchen by now, preparing the dinner they would eat together that day. Instead, she was missing.

Justin sighed. He should have known something like this would happen. This was Mary Ellen all over. Spontaneous, unreliable. He wasn't even all that surprised, he realized.

How could she do this to him? he wondered. Standing him up on a date was one thing, but disappearing before they were due to be published? With no explanation? She could have at least *talked* to him.

Part of him worried that perhaps they were judging her too harshly, that perhaps she really had gone for a walk that morning and she'd fallen or something, into a ditch or gulley, somewhere they hadn't looked.

He shook his head at himself. That was unlikely, he knew. They had scoured the area.

It wasn't even the fact that his fiancée had run off on him. In fact, if Justin were being truly honest with himself, he was a little relieved. He hadn't been quite sure about Mary Ellen, and here was vindication for that feeling, after all. But no, it was the *humiliation* of it, the deceit. Perhaps it wouldn't be so bad if his mother hadn't already told the neighbors about the wedding, but she had.

He slumped in his chair. He knew it was no good feeling sorry for himself, that sooner or later he would have to pick himself up and get on with his life, but that time just wasn't today.

Chapter Eleven

Rebecca slept badly that night, mostly due to Esther's snoring and occasional talking in her sleep. She hadn't moved her cot back into the girls' room as she'd hoped she be able to. Instead, Esther had insisted she stay. Rebecca understood why, of course. The old woman was afraid of falling off the bed again. *Rebecca* was afraid of Esther falling again. Still, spending even more time with Esther was difficult, and Esther insisted now that Rebecca go to bed when she did, so Rebecca wouldn't wake her up when she came in.

So Rebecca had lain in bed awake for hours, tired but unable to sleep until the middle of the night. She'd woken early, though, and managed to dress quietly enough so she didn't wake Esther.

When she returned from a short morning walk, Esther was

beginning to wake, and Rebecca saw to it that she had her sponge bath and was dressed neatly. She led Esther downstairs for breakfast, and helped Debbie slice bread and fruit, and entertained Ross while the children sat at the table, waiting.

The only ones not present were John and Ellen—Debbie told her they'd gotten up early to help the Schmuckers with their sheep. Harry complained about that. He seemed to think he should have gone over to help, too, but his mother told him sharply that if he'd gotten up on time, he might have.

"Perhaps you can help later," Rebecca suggested. The Schmuckers had over forty sheep, she knew, so they might need other help sometime soon.

No quicker had she spoken than Ellen and John came into the kitchen. They were both dirty but looked in good spirits.

After the two of them had washed up, everyone sat around the table for a family breakfast. It was pleasant, Rebecca thought, as everyone chattered away. Even Esther seemed to be in a better mood than usual. Rebecca wondered what her family was chatting about that morning. Did they miss her?

"I have something to tell you later," Ellen said, leaning into Rebecca a little, her voice low so no one else could hear.

Rebecca looked at her for a moment, wondering what she would go on about now. Ellen sounded so serious. But then, it *had* to be about Justin and Mary Ellen, didn't it?

After breakfast, Rebecca helped clear the table and *red* up the kitchen. She had decided to stay on sewing duty that morning, so she could be near Esther and watch the youngest two children while the rest of the Fretzes did the other chores.

Ellen found Rebecca at the top of the stairs, a small basket of clothes that were in need of repair held under her arm.

"What did you want to tell me?" Rebecca asked the girl. She hoped it wasn't anything too terrible.

"Mary Ellen's run off with an *Englischer*. That's why she and Justin weren't published on Sunday."

Rebecca's jaw dropped; she could barely believe it. Who would choose an *Englischer* over Justin? Who would choose anyone over Justin? Rebecca didn't know this Mary Ellen, but she had to conclude the woman was a fool.

"I know. I couldn't believe it either at first. It's a shame. I quite liked Mary Ellen, but I don't suppose I'll see her again now. Well, maybe in the shop, if she didn't run away from her job, too."

Rebecca shook her head. "It sounds like she's not really someone you want to be associating with anyway."

"*Ach*, she's all right. She's not, like, a bad person. She's quite nice, really, just... She's always had her own ideas about things. But then, she'll be shunned I s'pose, so I won't be able to talk with her anyway."

"Mary Ellen has left her entire life behind. I realize that I don't know her, I've never even met her, but I feel sorry for her."

Ellen looked distressed at her words. "You're right," she said. "But maybe she'll change her mind and come back one day."

"Maybe," Rebecca said, although she personally thought it unlikely. Leaving the church wasn't an easy thing to do, she thought, and if Mary Ellen ever came back, it would be in disgrace. No one would trust her again. Certainly not Justin.

Justin. The poor man. His fiancée had left him for an *Englischer*, the very day they were due to be published. He had to be feeling terrible.

Poor Justin, she thought again. But perhaps he'd had a lucky escape. Who on earth would leave Justin for *anyone*, let alone an *Englischer*? She shook her head to herself as she descended the stairs. That Mary Ellen really was a fool.

Justin couldn't help feeling like all eyes were on him. And indeed, it did seem that everyone was staring at him. Church was at the Schmuckers' house that Sunday, so at least he could make a quick escape afterward, if needed. How many people had his mother told about his engagement? Not many, she'd told him that morning, only Debbie Fretz, but who had Debbie told?

He shook his head. He knew Debbie. She liked to *hear* gossip, but rarely spread it around. He was being paranoid, he decided. Yes, a few people might have known he was involved with Mary Ellen, but he doubted they knew how far that involvement ran.

He braced himself and walked toward the open door of the Schmucker's home, leaving *Mamm* and *Dat* outside to finish their talk with the Farmers.

He was almost to the porch when a familiar voice halted him. "*Gut* morning, Justin," Rebecca said, her voice light and sweet, friendly.

Justin wondered if *she* knew. Most likely, but then what did it matter, he supposed. Whether people knew or didn't know wouldn't change the fact that Mary Ellen had left him for an *Englischer*. He was being prideful, he knew, but he couldn't help it.

He tipped his hat to Rebecca. "*Gut* morning."

"I haven't seen you in a while," she commented. "I hope you're keeping well."

He nodded. "I am, thank you." His words felt stiff and overly formal.

"Perhaps it's not my place to ask," she began, and Justin braced himself for whatever probing question might come next, "but perhaps you'd like to come for dinner tomorrow night? Debbie suggested it, so it's not all my idea. Oh, she'll probably ask you or your parents later on as well, so I shouldn't have overstepped, but ... well, it might be nice."

Justin smiled. It *would* be nice, he thought. It had been two weeks since he'd made an effort to socialize with anyone, and the Fretzes were just next door—he could make an excuse and leave pretty quickly if he felt inclined.

"That would be right nice," he said. "Although, I'll wait for Debbie's invitation."

Rebecca blushed—it was quite becoming on her, he thought, and smiled. "Yes," she agreed. "You should do that. And don't tell her I asked you first."

He laughed. "Yes, we wouldn't want to incur her terrible wrath, now, would we?"

Rebecca laughed at that. The idea of Debbie being wrathful was ridiculous. Justin didn't think he'd ever seen Debbie so much as mildly irritated, although perhaps she just hid it extremely well.

It was time to go in, then, and Justin took his seat.

Preaching service was a comfort that day. Here he was, surrounded by his community, family and friends, under the eyes of *Gott*. Where was Mary Ellen now? He wondered. What did she have in her life, now that she'd left all this behind? One man, and that was all. What would happen to her if it ended with him?

He knew he shouldn't worry about her—she'd lied to him, betrayed him—but he couldn't help it. He realized now she'd never been right for him, but that didn't change the fact that he *had* loved her. Perhaps it was best for him that she'd left, but was it best for *her?* He couldn't say—she'd never confided in him, never told him the truth. He was as much in the dark about her relationship with the *Englischer* as anyone else around here.

He tried to push thoughts of Mary Ellen to the back of his mind, and concentrate on the service, on the bishop's words and on the hymns they sang. Singing was a relief, like expelling something from him, opening himself up to something new. He felt every word, every note.

Perhaps, he thought, this wasn't just the end of something, it could also be the beginning of something else. But what that something else might be, he had no idea.

Chapter Twelve

Justin had known this day would come around, but it didn't make it hurt any less. It was the day of his would-be wedding. He should be standing in front of his friends and family right now, declaring his love for Mary Ellen, and her declaring her love for him. Instead, he was on his knees on the cold earth, a hammer in one hand and a nail held in his mouth, fixing loose panels in the chicken coop. Like it was just any other day.

He took the nail from his mouth and held it against the wood, then hammered it in. The wood cracked, and he groaned under his breath, letting the hammer drop to the ground with a *thump*.

He leaned back, hands curling into fists against his thighs. He breathed out, then in, slowly. *Gott,* he prayed silently. *Please help me to fight this anger. I need to let go.* He couldn't stay angry and hurt forever, he knew, but it was hard.

It didn't matter than he hadn't been quite sure about marrying Mary Ellen. It didn't matter that it was probably, all in all, for the best if he hadn't. The fact was that he'd made a commitment to her, and he'd meant to keep it. She, on the other hand, had made the same commitment and run off anyway, without a word, like he'd meant nothing to her. He'd loved Mary Ellen, but now he wondered if she'd ever loved him at all. Had it all been a lie? How long had she been seeing this *Englisch* fellow? It wasn't right.

Tomorrow, he told himself, would be better. Today, he would just have to try to put things out of his mind. Right now, he thought, he would find a new piece of wood, and he would finish this chicken coop—without any more groaning.

He got to his feet and was about to head to the barn to find more wood, when he spotted a figure in the distance, coming closer. It was Rebecca, he thought, although he couldn't quite tell from here. Part of him wanted to go over and speak with her, but another part wanted to hide, to see and speak to no one. He didn't much want to deal with other people today. He had more than enough on his mind. So instead, he headed in the other direction, toward the barn.

When he emerged with a new panel of wood, however, Rebecca was closer, almost at the fence. He was closer to the fence, too, and he could see her quite clearly now, no longer just a black and white blur but a woman. He waved to her, just to be polite, and she waved back, then beckoned him over.

He sighed and turned away from her. Hopefully, she would think he just hadn't seen. He didn't want to talk to Rebecca today, as nice as she was. He got the feeling lately that she pitied him, and he didn't want that, and certainly not today. So he ignored her, and returned to the chicken coop. It wasn't the only thing that needed fixing today, he thought bitterly. But the rest, he supposed, would take time.

The post came a little earlier than usual that morning. Rebecca brought it in for the family after her morning walk and set the letters down on the table. She was surprised when she did so to find one addressed to her. It was in her mother's handwriting, and she ripped it open eagerly, scanning through it quickly for any news.

Everyone was well, her mother wrote, preparing for Christmas and missing Rebecca; although, of course she said they would have their own little celebration when she got back, so there was that to look forward to. And there was news of Mary Joan, too. Her mother had heard from Mary Joan's mother that she was courting none other than the schoolteacher, Daniel Shrock.

Rebecca stared at those words. Were they true? she wondered. Mary Joan had never made any mention of courting Mr. Shrock, but then perhaps they had only gotten together recently...

She found, though, that she wasn't jealous of Mary Joan the way she might have been a few weeks ago. Instead, the news only made her sad that she wasn't there. She should have heard the news from Mary Joan herself. They should be sitting in the old barn, eating cookies and discussing the courtship like best friends, the way they'd talked about boys when they were younger.

Rebecca found that Daniel Shrock was no longer the object of her own affections. Had too much time passed? Perhaps distance did not make the heart grow fonder, after all. Or was it that someone else had taken that place in her heart and her mind? She frowned. She shouldn't think like that. But Justin...

He was kind and good, quiet and thoughtful, so down-to-earth. But it would never happen, she decided. It was terrible timing and besides, he was from Baker's Corner, Indiana, and she was from Land's Creek, Illinois. As welcoming as people had been to her, she couldn't imagine ever moving here. But she was getting carried away. She and Justin had never spoken like that and never would.

Rebecca sighed, read the letter through one more time, then folded it up and slotted it back into its envelope. She would write Mary Joan later that afternoon, she decided, and her mother as well.

She took a seat beside Esther in the sitting room and took up the knitting she'd begun earlier in the week. She wanted to make gifts for her family back home as well as for the Fretzes, who had been so good to her these last weeks.

"What's with the face?" Esther asked her sharply. "I thought hiring a young girl would brighten things up a bit but look at you. It's almost Christmas and you look as though you're about to attend a funeral."

"I do?" Rebecca blinked. She hadn't realized she'd looked so glum.

"*Jah*, you do."

"Well, let's hope it isn't your funeral," Rebecca said, far too sharply. She wasn't sure where the words had come from, and they shocked her. She was about to apologize, when Esther laughed, a throaty cackle.

"Oh, it may well be at that, but I don't suppose you would look quite so sad if it were."

"Don't say that," Rebecca told her. "What would I do with myself if you were gone? You know I can't abide having too much free time on my hands."

Esther laughed again. "Well, I'm sure I certainly help with that."

Rebecca smiled. She hadn't expected Esther, of all people, to be capable of lifting her spirits, but she couldn't deny that she had.

Chapter Thirteen

Rebecca couldn't help but be a little excited at the notion of Justin driving her to town. She had barely spoken to him since he'd come to dinner a few days ago, and she wanted to see how he was doing. He was, she thought, the one friend she had in Baker's Corner.

She gathered the two letters she had written to her mother and Mary Joan and placed them in her basket. She wouldn't linger in town too long, she decided, just long enough to post the letters and to buy wool and thread for her gift-making, and some flour for the last of the Christmas baking.

Justin arrived a little earlier than he'd said he would, but she was ready. He helped her up onto the buggy seat, ever the gentleman, and bid her a good morning. He sounded tired, like he hadn't slept all that well, and Rebecca worried at that.

She decided not to draw attention to it, however, or to ask if he was well. Instead, she said, "What are you getting up to in town today?"

"I have to go to the feed store and buy some nails. Nothing terribly exciting, I'm afraid, but then, I think I'm over excitement for a while."

Rebecca nodded. She could understand that. Mary Ellen had proved unreliable, and she didn't think Justin was the sort of person who enjoyed drama. He was far too even for that.

"Perhaps you'd like to come by for lunch later?" she asked him. "I know everyone would be pleased to have you round."

"Thank you," he said, "But I've a lot to be getting on with."

"Okay," she said, faltering at his cool tone. "Well, whenever you'd like. I know everyone would be pleased to see you any time."

He nodded at that but didn't say anything back.

Rebecca bit her lip. Had she overstepped a boundary somewhere? She wasn't sure. Justin didn't seem quite like himself today, not as warm toward her. It was possible he was still processing the ordeal with Mary Ellen, but what had that to do with her and lunch at the Fretzes? She fell quiet after that, and they rode the rest of the way into town in silence.

Once she'd posted her letters and done the small amount of shopping she'd needed to do, Justin was already waiting for her at the end of the street. She climbed up into the buggy and smiled at him. He didn't smile back.

"Did you get everything you needed?" she asked.

He nodded. "Did you?"

"I did," she said, injecting some cheer into her voice that she didn't really feel. Why was he being so cold? Was he just in a bad mood, or had she done or said something to offend him?

"Wonderful," he said, his tone still dry and cool.

He tugged on the reins to urge the mare into motion, and the buggy lurched forward.

Rebecca searched her mind for something to say, anything that would break the silence that had fallen around them.

Just out of town, a deer sprang across the road, and the mare gave a start, shying to the right. Justin soothed her and tugged on the reins to get her back on the road. For a moment, Rebecca didn't think the horse was going to obey, but then she calmed, and fell back into step again.

"Goodness," Rebecca said, "I thought we were going to be headed off the road for a second there."

"So did I," Justin admitted. "But Bessie's never let me down yet. Just a crisis of confidence on my part, I suppose."

"Well, if I were in her place, I would have been a bit startled too," Rebecca said. "In truth, I *was* a bit startled."

"I can't imagine you as a horse," Justin commented, his tone still dry.

Rebecca laughed, startled. "Well, I'm more or less a cart horse for old Esther."

"Oh, come on, it's not that bad," Justin said. "You're probably more like her faithful farm dog."

Rebecca raised her eyebrows. "I think you should stop comparing me to dogs and horses now, before I get quite offended."

"*Ach*, sorry," Justin muttered. "I was just—"

Rebecca cut him off. "Besides, Esther hates dogs. She'd never let one in her home."

Justin chuckled. "A horse it is. Although I'm amazed you manage to fit through her door."

Rebecca gave her best impression of a horse's whinny, and Justin laughed freely. He shook his head, still chuckling.

"What have you done to me?" he asked. "I don't think I've laughed this hard in..." He fell quiet for a second. "Well, in a while."

Rebecca filled in the gaps. He meant since Mary Ellen had left, she thought, or maybe a bit before that. The observation made her feel ill at ease, and they rode the rest of the way in even deeper silence.

Justin dropped her off at the end of the Fretzes driveway and bid her a good day. His tone was more pleasant than it had been earlier than morning, Rebecca was happy to note.

She entered the house and headed for the kitchen, to put away the jam and potatoes she'd bought in town at Debbie's request. She found the whole family around the table, eating a late lunch of bread, cold meats, and cheese. Their faces looked solemn, and Rebecca faltered, unsure. Had something happened?

"Ah, Rebecca," Esther said, turning to look at her. Her voice crackled, slightly rasping. "You should know I've decided to return home early. We'll be leaving the day after tomorrow."

The day after tomorrow? It was still a week until Christmas.

"But—" Rebecca started, but Esther cut her off.

"I've made up my mind," she said sternly, and Rebecca knew then that there was no arguing with her, nor even questioning her decision. At least, she thought, she would get to see her family at Christmas. And even if Esther didn't spend Christmas with hers, she had gotten these last weeks with them.

John looked disappointed, though, and so did the children. Debbie's face was more sympathetic, Rebecca thought, as she sat down to join them for lunch.

When she asked Esther about it later, Esther was still reluctant to explain her reasons, but eventually she said, "I'm old, and I'm dying. Dying happens in a funny sort of way. You wouldn't understand that, being such a young little thing, but I've seen people die. It happens slowly at first, and then fast, all at once. I'd prefer to die in my own home. Not here."

"You're not dying," Rebecca argued.

Esther scoffed at her. "What would you know? You don't live in this body. I do. We're leaving, and that's final. Honestly, I'd have thought you'd be glad."

Rebecca would have thought she'd be glad, too. In fact, her disappointment at the news surprised her.

"It's up to you," she told Esther. "I can't say I won't be pleased to see my family at Christmas." Still, she thought, there was one person she wouldn't see at Christmas—Justin.

Rebecca rose early the next morning to pack her and Esther's things. By the time she was finished, the rest of the household was awake, all except Esther, who Rebecca left to sleep a little longer.

She found Debbie and the children in the kitchen, some of the baked goods they'd prepared for Christmas still thawing on the counter.

"We're going to have Christmas early," Debbie announced to Rebecca. "Since Esther won't be with us on the actual day."

Bobby turned to Rebecca, his eyes wide and full of glee. "Two Christmases!" he said. "We never had *two* before!"

Rebecca smiled at him. "Well, this is a special year," she told him. "We should make the most of it."

She would miss these children, she thought. She would miss this house. Over the last weeks, it had become familiar to her, and she couldn't deny that it was much more welcoming than Esther's own home, even if Rebecca didn't have much space to herself. This house was full of warmth and life, possibly even more than her own family's home while she was growing up.

"What can I do to help?' she asked, and Debbie quickly put her to work.

They spent the morning preparing food—Harry and Ellen helping John to pluck and gut the chicken they would roast, while Rebecca and Bobby cut vegetables. Debbie was in charge of the baking, and the younger two children mostly just watched and made a mess.

Rebecca laughed as Ross stuck a thin slice of carrot up his nose. She quickly leaned over and pulled it out before he could do any damage. He grabbed the piece of carrot out of her hand and shoved it in his mouth before she could stop him, crunching loudly.

"Ew, gross!" Ellen said loudly, and Ross just grinned, his teeth flecked with little orange pieces.

Rebecca stifled another laugh and tried to focus on her work.

When it was time for Esther to get up, Rebecca helped wash her and get her dressed. Esther was less grumbly than usual, Rebecca was glad to note, once Rebecca had told her about the day's early Christmas celebrations.

"John's such a good boy," Esther told her. "Always so thoughtful."

Rebecca agreed. "I think he met a *gut* match with Debbie," she said.

Esther frowned. "She's not so awful," she begrudged. "Even if she *did* steal my boy away from me."

Rebecca laughed. "You make her sound like some wicked kidnapper."

"Why do you think they have so many children?" Esther said.

Rebecca gaped, shocked, and then laughed again. "Esther, you're terrible!" she said.

"That's one benefit of old age," Esther told her. "When you get to my age, you no longer care what anyone thinks of you, and you can say more or less what you want."

Rebecca shook her head, smiling.

They went downstairs together, Rebecca's arm looped through Esther's for support, Esther clinging to the wooden railing with her other hand.

Chapter Fourteen

Once most of the food was in the oven, Rebecca sat down to finish wrapping the last of her small gifts. For the Fretz family, she'd bought a nice puzzle. For Esther, she'd gotten a book, by one of Esther's favorite authors. She hesitated before wrapping her last gift. She didn't want to seem too forward, but Justin had been good to her here, a friend, she thought. Perhaps it was too much, though... It was only a little thing, a new pair of wool gloves. She'd noticed last week that his had holes in them.

She decided she would have to go now to give them to him. Any later, and she would be too involved with the Fretzes' Christmas, or become timid and never give the gift to him at all. If he wasn't in, she would simply leave it on his doorstep, which might be a better idea anyway.

She shook her head at herself. She really needed to stop overthinking everything.

She felt nervous, standing on the Raber's porch, waiting for someone to answer the door. When it opened, she breathed a sigh of relief. Justin stood in the doorway, his clothes neat and clean, strands of dark blond hair curling about his ears.

"Oh, Rebecca," he said, surprised. "*Gut* afternoon. What brings you here?"

She forced a smile, trying to swallow with the tightness in her throat. "I'm leaving early tomorrow," she said. "I wanted to say *gut*-bye, and to give you this." She held out the gift, wrapped in simple brown paper and string.

"Oh," he said, and she noticed a hint of disappointment in his voice. He took the gift. "Thank you. Although, I'm sorry you have to go so soon. I thought you were staying for Christmas."

"I was," Rebecca told him. "Esther changed her mind. She wants to go home."

"Why the change of heart?"

Rebecca shook her head. "She wants to be in her own home for Christmas." It was only half the truth, but there was no need to discuss Esther's concerns with Justin.

"That's a shame," he said. " I suppose you'll be glad to be

home for Christmas, too. It's probably a bit strange, being here and away from everyone you know at this time of the year."

"It's not been as terrible as I had thought," she said with a small smile. "Everyone's been very nice here."

"I'm glad. Um, I'm afraid I didn't get you a gift in return."

Rebecca shook her head. " It's only a small thing."

"May I write you?" he asked.

Rebecca resisted the urge to gape at him. Instead, she nodded.

She gave him her address, and he thanked her again for the gift. She walked away feeling rather strange, torn between sadness at leaving and hope at the idea of him writing her. She was leaving but she had that, at least.

Rebecca and Esther left early that morning, the sky still a dark blue, the sun just rising in the sky. The Fretz family saw them off at the door, the children waving goodbye. Although Rebecca had never wanted to come to Baker's Corner, she couldn't help but feel a little sad to be leaving so soon. The prospect of Christmas here hadn't really been so terrible after all, although she couldn't deny she would be glad to be home, to see her own friends and family. She had only been gone four weeks, but from the sound of her mother's letter, there was a lot to catch up on.

It was a tiring journey back to Land's Creek, but Rebecca found she slept almost as much as Esther. She had gone to bed too late the previous night, too busy listening to everybody talking, to notice the time.

But soon enough, they were home, and Rebecca felt a sense of elation at the familiar landscape—the roads she rode and walked every day, the farmhouses occupied by people she knew.

When they arrived back at Esther's house, Rebecca helped her inside, prepared them both a hot broth, and began to unpack for the both of them. Rebecca slept well that night, and the morning she was awake bright and early, eager to head home and see her family.

Her mother embraced her when she answered the door, while Iris merely commented, "You missed us too much, then, sister?"

"Of course," Rebecca said. "I couldn't stay away. Not on Christmas. Although, in truth, it was Esther's decision to come back."

"Well, that's *gut*," her mother told her, "Because we have far too much work to do between just the three of us. The school presentation needs an extra pair of hands, too, if you have the time."

Rebecca was only too glad to be asked. Although her motives to help out before might have had something to do with Mr. Shrock, she was only too glad to help now. She knew Iris would be helping, and Mary Joan, and it would give her something else to do besides caring for Esther.

They sat in the sitting room for a while, talking about the goings on of Land's Creek over the last weeks and the preparations that needed to be made for Christmas.

Yes, Rebecca thought to herself. It was good to be home.

"He just asked me," Mary Joan told her as they sat in her family's kitchen, making Christmas decorations. They were alone, finally, and Rebecca had asked her about Daniel Shrock. "I just bumped into him at the market, and we got talking, and a few days later he asked if he could take me out. Obviously, I said yes." Her face fell for a moment. "I'm sorry, I know you liked him too, but, so did I, and how could I say no?"

Rebecca shook her head. "It's really fine," she told her friend. "After a few weeks away, I don't think I'm really very interested in him anymore, anyway. Although I *was* surprised when my mother wrote me about it."

"Well, I was a bit surprised, too," Mary Joan admitted. "But I won't lie to you—I'm very happy."

Rebecca smiled. "I'm happy you're happy."

"That makes me happy too." Mary Joan laughed.

Rebecca leaned across the table to grab the string and was caught off guard by Mary Joan's next words.

"What about you?" she asked. "You say you're no longer interested in Daniel. Does that mean there's someone else? Maybe someone you met in Baker's Corner?" She raised her eyebrows.

Rebecca stifled a laugh. Mary Joan was far too perceptive for her own good. But Rebecca found she didn't really want to discuss Justin with her. She had received one letter from him, the day after she'd returned home and hadn't even posted her reply yet. His letter indicated that he was maybe keen on her, but she wasn't sure. It was possible that they would never be anything more than friends and pen pals.

"You're far too nosey," she said instead, and Mary Joan laughed.

"Come on," she said. "I know you too well, Rebecca, and you're a terrible liar. Even a terrible white liar. You can't hide anything from me."

Rebecca raised her eyebrows. "Oh, really?" she said. "Then where have I hidden your Christmas present?"

Mary Joan rolled her eyes. "*You* are my Christmas present," she said. "Truly, I'm so glad you're home. I've missed you."

Rebecca smiled. "I've missed you, too," she admitted, happiness swelling through her. If anything came from her friendship with Justin, she thought, Mary Joan would be the first person she'd tell.

Chapter Fifteen

Justin read Rebecca's letter for the third time, happiness blossoming in his chest at her words. It was a rather matter-of-fact letter, which of course he'd expected from Rebecca. She talked about how busy she was with the Christmas baking and making decorations for her family's and Esther's homes, and for the school presentation. She talked about her family, and about her friend, Mary Joan, and Justin could almost see those people in his mind's eye, like he was getting a little glimpse of Land's Creek, without ever having been there.

He was pleased to note that despite how busy she'd been the last couple of days, she'd still made time to write to him. Mary Ellen had rarely ever made time for him. She saw him only if she had time but had never really prioritized him. Not that he was comparing the two women—that wouldn't be quite proper, he told himself.

He wished he could see Rebecca and hear her voice, but the letter was almost as good. The letter, he could keep, and read over again and again. He sat down at the small writing desk in the study and pulled paper and pen toward him. He paused for a moment, suddenly unsure what to write. And then it came to him. What did he *really* want to say to Rebecca? The answer was simple, really. He smiled to himself, forcing back his nerves, and began to write.

Christmas day dawned clear, and Rebecca could feel the sun on her face as she scattered feed for the chickens outside.

Inside, she checked the food defrosting on the counters. She'd gotten the baked goods out the night before, but they weren't quite thawed just yet. Still, in only an hour or two, they would be ready.

She went into Esther's room then to wake her, drawing back the curtains and laying a hand gently on her shoulder. She might have left her to sleep, but there was a preaching service to attend.

Esther grumbled and rubbed at her eyes. She looked very small today, Rebecca thought sadly, bony and vulnerable. Rebecca didn't like that. Esther had always seemed to her stern and formidable, especially when she was speaking her mind.

At breakfast, Esther watched her for a moment. "I don't need you here today," Esther told her. "After church, you can bring me home and then have the rest of the day off. Spend Christmas with your family."

Rebecca bit her lip. "Are you sure?" she asked. She didn't like the idea of Esther spending Christmas at home alone, but she wasn't about to turn down the chance to spend most of the day with her family, instead of just a few hours at dinner time.

Esther waved a bony hand. "*Jah, jah*. Of course. You're a nuisance. I want some peace today."

Rebecca frowned. There was no need to be harsh—although of course, that was Esther's way.

"Very well then," she said, a little put out. She'd never been described as a 'nuisance' before, not even by Esther.

After church, Rebecca took Esther home, made sure there was ample food and that Esther had everything she needed, and then left, the basket hanging from her arm full of Christmas presents her family. She had left Esther's present on the sitting room table, for her to open as she pleased, but she hadn't received one in return. Still, she could suppose that a full afternoon off was as good a gift as Esther could give her.

It was a wonderful Christmas, Rebecca decided, as she helped her mother and sister set out the dinner, with the sounds of child's laughter coming from the living room, where her brother and his wife were playing with their son. Still, Rebecca couldn't help but feel something wasn't quite right. Esther was alone on Christmas day, stuck in that gloomy old house with only her chickens and that half-wild ginger tabby for company. She had an idea, then, and asked her mother if it was all right.

"Of course," *Mamm* told her. "Go and speak to your *dat*. I'm sure he'll go."

Rebecca smiled and did as she said.

Half an hour later, Esther was seated in their sitting room, a quilt over her knees, a baby on her lap. After a few minutes, however, and an ear-splitting laugh from little Thomas, Esther grumbled, "Take him away."

Rebecca frowned, but picked Thomas up and set him back on his father's lap.

They exchanged gifts soon after that, and Rebecca was pleased to note Esther had thought to bring the gift Rebecca had left for her on the table.

She received books from her *Mamm* and *Dat*, a pair of deerskin gloves from Iris, a new pair of socks from James and Catherine, and from Esther, a shakily embroidered handkerchief. Rebecca couldn't have been more pleased, and she flung her arms around Esther, taking care not to be too rough with the woman.

"I love it," she said.

Esther waved her away. "Don't be silly," she said. "It's awful. I should have thrown the ugly thing away, but I didn't want to start again."

Rebecca smiled. "It's beautiful, and besides, what do you care if it's not perfect, you know what a handkerchief is used for."

Iris giggled, and their mother said, sharply, "Rebecca!"

Rebecca tried to look contrite but couldn't quite manage it. Esther cackled, and the old woman's laugh was music to her ears.

They ate dinner together then, a feast of roasted chicken and vegetables, with mashed potatoes and gravy. Afterward, when Iris and Rebecca and Catherine were clearing the plates, her mother pulled her to one side. "Daughter, I'm afraid I forgot," she said. "Your father checked Esther's mail while he was there, and this was in there for you."

"Oh," Rebecca said, quickly taking the letter from her. "I completely forgot to check the mailbox yesterday. I was just so busy with everything else." She looked at the envelope, recognizing Justin's handwriting immediately.

She took the letter upstairs to open it in private and smiled to herself at the words inside. Justin wanted to visit her. And the very next week. That was so soon, she thought, but her heart felt full, like it was ready to burst. She would write to him as soon as she could, and tell him that of course, he should visit.

She went back downstairs, feeling as though this might have to be the best Christmas ever.

Justin tried to push away his nerves as he approached the white-painted house. Chickens clucked around him, and a ginger tabby cat stretched and yawned, then abandoned its sleeping spot on the porch railing, disappearing around the side of the house with one last, disgruntled look back at him.

Justin hoped he wasn't being too forward. He'd meant to arrive next week, but how could he wait? He knew now what he wanted, what he'd wanted for weeks, but hadn't been able to admit to himself.

He stood on the porch and knocked on the door.

Rebecca was washing the dishes when the knock sounded at the door. She set the last plate on the draining board and wiped her hands on her apron.

"Expecting visitors?" Rebecca asked Esther as she passed the sitting room door.

"Visitors?" Esther grumbled. "Send them away."

Rebecca stifled a laugh and went to the door.

Her jaw dropped when she opened it. Standing there, his hat in his hands, his fingers moving over the brim nervously, was Justin.

"What on earth—" Rebecca started, then frowned. Had she read the date wrong? Had he meant to arrive this week, and not next, and she'd forgotten?

"My apologies," he started. "I know I asked to visit next week, but I was lying in bed last night, and, well... I just couldn't wait. I *had* to see you."

Rebecca stared at him, unsure of what to say. "My goodness," she finally uttered. "In that case, you better come inside."

"Thank you," he said, "but there's something I want to ask you first."

Rebecca felt suddenly nervous, and she bit her lip, waiting.

"I-I'd like to court you," he said. "I hope you agree, but... what I need most from you is an honest answer, so please, don't be afraid to tell me anything you think I might not want to hear."

"Justin," Rebecca said, a smile curving her mouth. "Of *course,* my answer is yes. I would like it very much if you were to court me. How could I not? Now, please, come in out of the cold, because I am absolutely freezing."

He laughed at that, and his hand brushed Rebecca's arm as he moved to come inside. They walked into the house together, and she heard Esther's voice calling out from the kitchen.

"Who was it? I hope you sent them away!"

The End.

Continue Reading...

Thank you for reading *Smitten at Christmas!* **Are you wondering what to read next?** Why not read *Homeless for Christmas?* **Here's a peek for you:**

"What's Will Helmuth doing here?" Nancy Springer asked. She gazed out the kitchen window of her cousin Doreen's farmhouse, overlooking the barn and outbuildings. She had no difficulty recognizing the handsome widower who lived on the farm bordering Doreen's land to the east.

"He offered to help me out around the farm when I injured my foot a while back this past spring, and he's continued to come around since then," the older woman replied.

Cousin Doreen was getting into her middle years and lived here alone, having never married. Besides that, she was a thin woman who barely stood over five feet tall. It was understandable that it would be difficult for her to complete all the chores on her own—even now that her injury had healed. Some of the heavier tasks would continue to be too much for her as she grew older.

"It's kind of him to help you," Nancy remarked.

She was surprised to learn about it, however. Not because Will Helmuth was the kind of man who would begrudge giving his aid to a neighbor. But because Nancy hadn't had any inkling of it before then, though she was a frequent visitor to her cousin's farmhouse when she needed a respite from her own troubles at home—a need that was becoming more and more common of late.

Nancy came here any time she needed a few minutes of peace away from the constant worries at her family's farm. They lived a few miles farther along the highway that led to the small town of Baker's Corner. She would have noticed if Will had been here during any of her previous visits.

Now, she watched as he crossed the barren yard and headed toward the back door of the farmhouse.

Patches of snow covered the ground from an early winter snowstorm that had blanketed the countryside the week before. And the dark clouds overhead heralded more snow to come before nightfall. Although it was only the beginning of December, winter came early to Indiana.

She lost sight of Will as he mounted the back porch, and a moment later a knock sounded on the kitchen door.

"I'll get it," she said when the older woman moved toward the door to answer it. Nancy hurried forward, not giving Doreen a chance to refuse.

The top half was the door was made up of several glass panes, and she could see the outline of Will's broad shoulders through the closed curtains.

VISIT HERE To Read More:

http://www.ticahousepublishing.com/amish-miller.html

Thank you for Reading

If you **love Amish Romance, Click Here**

https://amish.subscribemenow.com/

to find out about all **New Hannah Miller Amish Romance Releases! We will let you know as soon as they become available!**

If you enjoyed ***Smitten at Christmas,*** would you kindly take a couple minutes to leave a positive review on Amazon? It only takes a moment, and positive reviews truly make a difference. I would be so grateful! Thank you!

Turn the page to discover more Hannah Miller Amish Romances just for you!

More Amish Romance from Hannah Miller

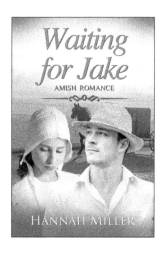

Visit HERE for Hannah Miller's Amish Romance

https://ticahousepublishing.com/amish-miller.html

About the Author

Hannah Miller has been writing Amish Romance for the past seven years. Long intrigued by the Amish way of life, Hannah has traveled the United States, visiting different Amish communities. She treasures her Amish friends and enjoys visiting with them. Hannah makes her home in Indiana, along with her husband, Robert. Together, they have three children and seven grandchildren. Hannah loves to ride bikes in the sunshine. And if it's warm enough for a picnic, you'll find her under the nearest tree!

CPSIA information can be obtained
at www.ICGtesting.com
Printed in the USA
LVHW051952101220
673847LV00017B/2617